On the darkest night of winter, can he bring light to her wounded heart?

THE STORM

Scarred by loss, Irina warrior Renata has held the world at a distance. Fighting the Grigori and protecting humanity are her goals, but her heart remains frozen to the bonds of family and love. Only one scribe, Maxim of Riga, has managed to see through Renata's armor.

On the darkest night of winter, in the halls of her ancestral home, Renata is forced to face her past. Can a fierce storm and a stubborn scribe coax her back to life, or will she retreat into duty forever?

with bonus novella SONG FOR THE DYING

When a letter arrives from a remote scribe house in Latvia, Leo and Max must return to their childhood home to face the father and grandfather who raised them.

The past is inescapable, but can it be overcome? Is it possible to build a future of happiness from a foundation of pain?

The Storm and *Song for the Dying* are novellas in the Irin Chronicles, a romantic fantasy series by Elizabeth Hunter.

THE STORM

IRIN CHRONICLES BOOK SIX

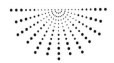

ELIZABETH HUNTER

This book is dedicated to
all those who are brave enough to choose love.

The Storm
Copyright © 2017
Elizabeth Hunter
978-1987554847

Cover: Damonza
Content Editor: Heather Monroe
Line Editor: Anne Victory
Proofreader: Linda, Victory Editing

This is a work of fiction. Names, characters, places, and incidents are either the products of the author's imagination or used fictitiously, and any resemblance to actual persons, living or dead, or business establishments, organizations or locales is completely coincidental.

THE STORM

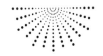

Scarred by loss, Irina warrior Renata has held the world at a distance. Fighting the Grigori and protecting humanity are her goals, but her heart remains frozen to the bonds of family and love. Only one scribe, Maxim of Riga, has managed to see through Renata's armor.

On the darkest night of winter, in the halls of her ancestral home, Renata is forced to face her past. Can a fierce storm and a stubborn scribe coax her back to life, or will she retreat into duty forever?

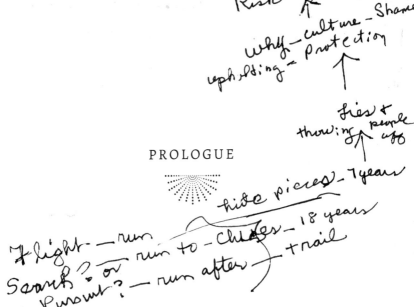

PROLOGUE

There was no road to the old house that sat on the edge of a mountain. An old and overgrown trail was the only path. It would take over an hour to hike in the heavy winter snow of the Dolomite Mountains. Even with the superior strength and stamina granted by his angelic blood, Maxim knew he'd be exhausted by the time he found her.

He'd parked his four-wheel drive in the closest town, cautiously following the directions of an old librarian a few villages farther south. Chasing rabbit trails to dead ends was commonplace at this point in his search, but Max knew he only needed one more piece of the puzzle.

He'd finally found a name for her hiding place. *Ciasa Fatima.*

It had taken him eighteen years to find that name. Eighteen years of lies and misdirection. Eighteen years of frustration. At this point, he didn't know if he wanted to find her from longing or sheer spite.

The librarian who gave him the name of the house was an ancient Ladin man who'd lived his entire life in Southern Tyrol and claimed to know the house Max was looking for. Once it had been the house of a great family, he claimed. They had a library to rival

Midwife kept notebook. She never talked.
*Then → Brown V Education. Thirro
the spirits. 6 years of peace.

the duke's! Strange people would come and go. Soldiers and noble-men. Beautiful women and visitors from foreign lands. There were stories and legends galore. Quiet

Then two hundred years ago, everything went quiet. There were no more visitors. No caravans or dignitaries. One hundred years passed before signs of life emerged. Change

These days, the house was rented out to discreet and very private travelers in the summer. No one knew how it was listed, and it couldn't be an easy place to stay. There was no electricity running up the mountain and probably no running water. But the meadows that surrounded it were worth the hike. The view, the old man remembered, was breathtaking.

In the winter, of course, it was vacant. No one wanted to brave the snow and ice of the cold Tyrolean winter on their own, especially not on a mountain slope like the one around Ciasa Fatima.

Except during the winter solstice.

For a few weeks in the middle of winter, villagers claimed that smoke came from the chimneys and lights glittered on the mountain. Whoever stayed at Ciasa Fatima didn't come down into the village.

This did not surprise Max.

There was no one better at hiding than Renata.

n. b.

*held a letter from county Super...

MAX CRESTED the last hill and stopped to breathe, making a note that high-altitude training was an area of his fitness that could be improved. He'd become accustomed to the lazy heat and balmy sea air of Istanbul. ELAINE = School Teacher of music

Perhaps there was a spell he could conjure for increased lung capacity. Maxim of Riga was an Irin scribe, and though most of his duties consisted of gathering strategic information for his watcher and other allies across the globe, he was still an accomplished practitioner of magic. All scribes had to be in order to wield the power

4

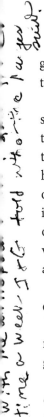

granted to them by their angelic forefathers. Male Irin harnessed their magic by writing. Female Irina used their voices.

For scribes, the most permanent spells—those for increased strength, stamina, eyesight, speed, and long life—were tattooed on their skin in intricate *talesm* unique to each warrior. Max had tattooed more than most, caught for years in a friendly rivalry with his cousin Leo. Both of them were young for their race at a little over two hundred years old, but they were massive men with intense focus who had spent the majority of their lives surrounded only by warriors. With a single brush of his thumb, Max could activate a dense web of magic on his skin, giving him a coat of living armor.

But none of that armor helped when it came to tracking down one elusive Irina.

The hike had taken twice as long as he'd anticipated, and darkness had already descended on the mountain. It didn't interrupt the grandeur of the view.

The house beyond the snow-covered meadow was just as the old man had described. A typical Ladin house, almost a perfect square of solid architecture that could withstand the fiercest storm. It was backed up to the mountain slope, possibly built into it. The bottom story was stone and plaster, the top was weather-aged wood. It was in good repair from the steep-sloped roof to the large porch that wrapped around the second story. Two outbuildings stood to the side—a low stone cottage and a larger barn that looked like it had once been a dairy.

Max started toward the house, breaking a path through two feet of solid snow. He could see lights in the distance; it was dark, and he was freezing cold. The chimney smoked, promising warmth if he could just make the last frozen yards.

A storm was coming in, and Max couldn't stop his smile. He couldn't have timed it better if he'd tried.

H<small>E BEAT ON THE DOOR</small>, but no one answered. "Renata!"

Nothing but silence, though he could hear someone inside.

"I know you're in there, and it's freezing out here. If you want me to keep the ass you seem so fond of, then you'd better let me in."

Still nothing.

This isn't like her.

Renata *never* ran from confrontation. Instincts on alert, Max turned the heavy brass knob.

The door swung open on silent hinges, and Max walked into a kitchen out of a Tyrolean postcard. It was nothing like he'd expect of Renata. An old stove glowed in the corner, and a round cake dotted with fruit cooled next to it. Cinnamon and sugar drifted on air filled with the sounds of soft accordion music from an old record player. A kerosene lamp was centered on the rustic wooden table, and stacks of cut wood lay piled along the far wall. Dozens of pine boughs hung from dark wooden rafters, and intricately cut paper stars decorated them.

Someone had decorated for Midwinter.

Max stepped into the room, immediately removing his snow-covered boots and heavy backpack. "Renata?"

"Max."

He followed the sound of her voice through the kitchen and into the large open area dominated by a central hearth. More pine boughs hung from the rafters. More stars. Cut crystal lamps with glowing beeswax candles lit the room. Snow had started to fall beyond the frost-covered windows.

Renata was sitting on the floor in front of the crackling fire, hair long and loose around her, dressed in an old-fashioned nightgown. She looked surprisingly young and more than a little vulnerable.

Max was struck dumb at the sight. If there was anyone more jaded and cynical than him, it was Renata. But here she was, sitting in the middle of a snow-covered dream, her brown eyes locked on him as he slowly approached. She'd been crying. In her hands she clutched an old silver candelabra, the seven-branched kind the Irin people used to celebrate Midwinter, the longest night of the year, and the coming of new light and life.

What is this place?

Renata did not look happy to see him. Then again, he hadn't expected her to.

She asked, "How did you find this place?"

He knew she was angry, but he couldn't stop his smile. "It's only taken me eighteen years."

She stood, set the candelabra down, and reached for a robe on the chair beside her. She wrapped it around herself and stood tall. She was nearly as tall as Max. He loved that about her figure. Then again, he loved everything about her figure.

"I climbed the mountain to find you," Max said. "The snow—"

"You should go," she said. "You shouldn't have come here."

He caught her arm before she could walk away. "I'm not going anywhere."

With a whispered spell, she forced his hand away. Max backed up without thinking, his body obeying her magic even as his mind fought against it.

"We've already had this conversation," she said. "I'm not interested in repeating it."

"I wouldn't call that a conversation. You had your say. Now it's my turn."

"I didn't agree to that."

His temper spiked. "I tracked you down to the middle of nowhere. I hiked a mountain in two feet of fresh snow. I damn near froze my toes off to get here. You're going to hear me out."

Renata glanced out the window. "There's a storm coming."

"I know."

"Did you plan that?"

"Despite your obvious admiration for my magical prowess, I don't control the weather."

She refused to look at him. She walked to the kitchen and he followed her.

"Renata—"

"You can stay the night." She bent down to one of the cupboards in the kitchen and took out another lamp. "You'll leave in the morning."

"I don't agree to that."

She continued, "There's only one bedroom prepared, so—"

"That's fine. It certainly won't be the first time we've shared a bed."

"You can take the sofa in the living room." She lit the lamp and pulled her robe tighter. "I told you. No more. There is no electricity here. You can use the lamp on the table if you need light around the house. They put in pumps last year, so there is plumbing inside now. If you want hot water, you'll have to boil it yourself. The toilet is down the hall."

Max took a deep breath, forcing back the anger that wanted to take the reins. They did this to each other. They had been sporadic lovers, sparring partners, and wary allies for eighteen years. No one knew how to push his buttons like Renata.

"You made a decision," he said quietly, "that you decided was for *my* best interests—"

"You know I'm right."

"—but you never consulted me."

Max stepped closer until his lips were inches from hers. He could feel her energy, the pulsing, powerful magic that drew him. Max didn't need a fire when he had her. She'd thawed out the cold heart of him, and then she'd had the audacity to take that heat and life away.

"I'll sleep on the sofa," he said. "But I'll see you in the morning."

SOMETIME IN THE dead of night, she came to him. Part of him knew she would. Their attraction was a force of nature and always had been.

The couch was too small for his large frame, so he'd rolled out a pallet on the rug in front of the fire. With the thick wool rug, heavy blankets, and down pillows from the sofa, it was far from the most uncomfortable place he'd slept.

Renata slipped under the blankets and scooted her back to his chest. "Don't say anything."

He didn't. Max knew better than to question her need when he felt it just as keenly.

She laid her head on his bicep, using his arm as her pillow. Max combed his fingers through the length of her hair, bringing the weight of it to his lips so he could feel the satin against his skin. Then he laid his head on the down-filled pillow and tucked his arm around her waist, fitting her body to his.

This is how it should be. This is how it should always be.

"Rest with me tonight," he whispered. "Wake with me in the morning. I'm not going anywhere. Neither are you. It's time to finish this."

CHAPTER ONE

South Tyrol, Italy
Summer, 1810

Renata tried hiding her smile as she watched the fine cut of Balien's hips as he led them up the mountain. Her parents lagged behind them, no doubt having paused to debate the manuscript they were writing together. They'd been arguing over a minor point since they'd left the village.

Balien looked over his shoulder and caught her gaze. "Shame-less," he said with a slight smile.

"Can you blame me?" Renata asked, glancing again at his firm backside. "You are a fine specimen of a man, Balien of Damascus."

He paused and let Renata catch up to him, hooking an arm around her waist and bringing her lips to his. "And you are the most beautiful of women." He kissed her. "How was I so lucky to find my peace in you?"

"You had to fight wars, traverse deserts, and climb mountains to find me." Renata laid her head on his broad shoulder. "I don't think luck had anything to do with it. You've earned your peace."

"When so many of my brothers fell around me?" He brushed his lips over her forehead. "It was only by the blessing of heaven that I survived to find my *reshon*."

Her heart swelled at the sound of his soul voice whispering within him, resonant as a bell struck in the clear mountain air. Renata closed her eyes and listened. *This is the greatest joy. Nothing is more beautiful than this.*

She'd lived a quiet life with her parents, but a happy one. Trained as an Irina archivist, she spent countless hours listening to her mother and learning the songs the women of their race perfected to pass along magic, history, and learning. Renata knew songs to make the earth and the womb more fertile. She knew songs to heal sickness and fever. She knew magic that could move the very mountain their home sat upon, creating protected caves in the hills to house the library where her father and his brothers stored the written knowledge they were tasked to protect.

Balien, on the other hand, had traveled the whole world. He'd come to the mountain the summer before, a weary warrior who'd fought too long without respite. Balien of Damascus was a warrior of an ancient order, his blood a rich mixture of the Near East, Northern Africa, and Europe. Like his blood, his looks were a striking combination that had fascinated Renata and drawn her attention at first glance.

His people were not the rulers of their territory, but they were renowned for two things: skill in battle and magic in healing. Balien was a Rafaene scribe, descended from the offspring of the archangel Rafael and gifted in healing arts.

A blessing and a curse for one destined to wage war. Most Rafaenes took regular breaks from battle against the Grigori—the descendants of fallen angels who preyed on humanity—to rest and heal their spirit. It was accepted and necessary.

But when Renata had met him, Balien hadn't taken a break in three decades. Forced into respite, he'd come to Renata's beloved mountains, acting as a courier for a scribe house in Jerusalem. A tedious job for a warrior feared by demons on three continents.

But Renata had met him, and she knew. Balien had taken one look at her and been struck dumb. All they'd needed was a single touch to feel their connection.

Reshon.

Destined by heaven, Balien was the man designed to complete Renata's soul, as she'd been created for him. Once they mated, they would live in each other's subconscious, connected by dreams, even if their paths took them to opposite corners of the earth. It was the mating that every Irin dreamed of.

She rested her head against his heart, listening to the strong beat of it as her parents' distant voices grew nearer.

"... the conflict between the written and the oral versions of the tale only confirm—"

"That there is no conflict?" her mother asked with a laugh. "Why must everything be so rigid, Giorgio? Scribes must write everything down and file everything in neat boxes. That is not how Irina history is kept."

"Which makes it less exact," Giorgio said.

"Which makes your scrolls only words on a page," said her mother, Heidi. "They convey nothing of the meaning—the emotion—behind the history."

"And do you want *emotion* with your history?" Giorgio asked. "Is that necessary for learning?"

"Of course we do," Balien said quietly, interrupting him. "For the horror of war isn't captured by words, Father, but by the lament of a widow. The cries of a fallen brother. If we forget the emotion behind history, we have lost our souls."

Giorgio nodded deeply. "I see your point, my son."

"But you didn't see mine?" Heidi said. "It had to come from a soldier for you to listen?" She narrowed her eyes and stalked up the path, brushing past Balien as Giorgio ran after her.

"Heidi!" he cried. "That's not what I was trying to say. I was only..."

Their voices drifted in the distance as Renata bit her lips to hold in her laughter.

"They will be like this always," Balien said. "Won't they?"

Renata let herself laugh. "I'm afraid so."

He took her hand and tugged her along. "Ah, we can always take to the roads if it becomes too much."

"I can protect you," Renata said. "I have my staff."

Balien winked at her. "Thank heaven."

Despite his joking, she knew he adored her family. His own parents were formal and a bit distant. Not unloving, but it was not in their way to be familiar. The chaos and warmth of the library at Ciasa Fatima was welcome to him. It was a small library with only four or five families in residence at once. They were constantly running out of room for people in favor of making room for books, so rooms were constantly being added and construction never ceased. It was crowded and messy and highly unorganized in anything nonacademic.

And Renata thought it was glorious.

Her mother and father were the undisputed leaders of the small Irin community as others came and went, but those who left always came back to visit. Ciasa Fatima was a haven in the wilderness and free of the politics that often marked larger and more connected libraries.

They crested the last hill before the house and almost ran into Giorgio and Heidi.

"Father?" Balien asked. "What is it?"

Both her parents were frozen. Still as statues. They stared into the distance, and Renata could feel a deep surge of magic swirling around them.

Balien's eyes followed theirs and he pushed her behind him. "Renata, stay back." He drew out the twin silver daggers he always wore.

"Balien?"

Giorgio grabbed his own daggers and fell into step behind

Balien. For though every Irin male was tasked with the protection of wisdom and knowledge, every scribe was also a warrior, trained in the killing arts to protect the vulnerable.

"Mother?"

Heidi grabbed Renata's hand and gripped tight. "Raise your shields," she choked out, lifting the staff she used for walking and for fighting. "I don't understand. I don't understand."

Finally moving around her mother, Renata peered through the dense tree line along the meadow. She could see the house in the distance. For a second, everything seemed as it had before they'd left two weeks before on a trading trip.

But there was no smoke in the chimney. She could hear the milk cows lowing in pain. Goats and sheep wandered outside the pen, and not a single one of the shepherd dogs barked.

Renata lifted her shields, listening for the dozen familiar souls who shared their home.

Nothing.

"No." Renata started forward, but her mother grabbed her and held her back. "No!"

"Hush." Heidi slapped a hand over Renata's mouth. "Be quiet!"

Balien and Giorgio moved through the grass, her warrior so stealthy she barely saw him. She could see his magic ripple around him. The grass barely moved as they rushed through it. Both scribes ran in complete silence. They split near the fence that surrounded the compound and disappeared from view.

Renata lowered every shield, desperate to hear anything.

A few minutes later, the low keening of her *reshon*'s soul moved Renata to run. Her mother was only steps behind her.

She ran straight to the house. She could hear no one and nothing but her intended mate and her father.

No, no, no.

Bursting through the kitchen door, she saw signs of struggle. Saw upturned chairs and blackened pots on the stove. She saw spatters of blood and a staff broken in half by the stove.

15

To woke up & want to start the day = Love. Something one whom we love

The first clothes she saw were the crumbled garments of Werner, the small boy who loved feeding the goats.

"No!" She knelt by the bench at the kitchen table, her fingers trailing though the remains of gold dust he'd left as his tiny soul rose to heaven. "Mother!"

Heidi had bypassed the kitchen and ran into the large living room. Renata could hear her sobbing. Clutching Werner's small jacket, she rose and walked to the hearth.

More violence. More destruction.

More blood. More dust.

Empty clothes lay scattered around the room, some kicked askew and others lying neatly on the floor, as if their owners had simply set them out to wear in the morning. Renata wandered through the room in a daze. Her father rushed in and grabbed her mother, clutching her to his chest as they both wept. Renata had never heard her father weep like that. They were deep, gut-wrenching cries of grief and rage.

Every room had more empty clothes.

Every room had more dust. More blood. More horror.

Balien found Renata in the ritual room where the sacred fire of the library had been snuffed out. Linen robes from the two elders lay there, the scribe's robes bunched by the door, lying scattered in smears of blood. The Irina robes were drenched with it, as if someone had cut the elder singer's throat as she faced the fire.

"The elders," she muttered. "The children…"

Balien stared at her, his face blank. "Everyone is gone. The whole house reeks of sandalwood."

Sandalwood. The heady fragrance could only mean Grigori killers. Their mountain fortress had been invaded by the sons of the Fallen. Renata couldn't even imagine them being a target. They were a library. Balien was the only warrior here. Their community was made of old men and women. Scholars and dairymen and farmers. Children.

She couldn't fathom it. No, this was a bad dream. This was a horrible nightmare, and she'd wake up and Balien would be warm next to her in bed, and she would hear the songs from the kitchen and the children's laughter outside. The house would smell like cinnamon again, and the scribes and singers would be cheerfully arguing among themselves in the library.

Renata closed her eyes, but she didn't hear laughter when her legs went out from under her.

She only heard her father weeping.

Rome
Midwinter

RENATA WATCHED her mother light the candles with dead eyes. The songs that should have filled the house during the longest night of the year were absent. They hadn't baked the honeyed bread that filled the house with warmth. They'd bought plain bread from the human bakers and hid in the small house on the outskirts of Rome.

Balien had kept them alive through the Rending, but it had not been easy. They'd fled Ciasa Fatima the same night they found the remnants of their community. They'd hidden in caves in the mountains for weeks, only coming down when runners from Vienna reached the library.

It wasn't only their library. Irin communities around the world —even those across the ocean—had been destroyed by a burst of Grigori violence that had sprung up in the warm summer months. Northern warriors were desperately trying to reach Irin communities in the south, hoping to fortify their numbers before winter broke and Grigori attacked there too.

They'd had no word from Balien's family. Rumors were rampant that Irina centers of learning had been hit first and fiercest. Thousands had been killed. Children were slaughtered. The girls, in particular, were hunted like animals.

"What are we celebrating?" Renata asked quietly.

"The longest night." Her father put an arm around her mother and kissed the top of Heidi's head. "The nights will grow shorter from this one. Light will come again. The sun will shine, and our people will recover."

Balien didn't speak. He rarely spoke anymore. Though he still shared Renata's bed, they took little comfort from each other in their grief and uncertainty. Renata wished Balien was willing to go forward with their mating, but he refused until the situation had stabilized.

"It's not safe. Mating involves a transfer of power. We will both be weaker for a time. We need to be safe before we perform the ritual."

"It may never be safe," she said. "Will we never be mated?"

He said nothing.

"I know you fear—"

"You don't know what I fear," he said. "You've never been in war. You don't know the depravity the Grigori are capable of."

"Don't I?"

There were times when she felt him on the edge of her dreams, reaching out for her. It was the only thing that gave her hope. Though he'd marked her with his magic, they'd never claimed each other. Until they did, his walls could not be breached by her magic.

Renata reached out and took Balien's hand, linking their fingers together. She laid her head on his shoulder, and he kissed her forehead. The simple movement brought her to tears.

Her mother sang the songs quietly. Her father read from the scrolls he'd saved from the library. But when Balien and Renata took to bed that night in the small room at the top of the narrow house, joy was a stranger to her.

"Will we ever feel happy again?" she asked. "I can't imagine ever wanting to sing. Maybe it's better that we don't mate. If we mated, I might want children." Her throat closed with emotion. "And we should not bring children into this world. Not like this."

Balien turned to her and enclosed her in his embrace as she

cried. "Your father is right," he said, clutching her tightly. "We will smile again. We will sing again. We will recover from this, Renata."

She had no words. His reassurances rang hollow.

"I'm sorry I have been distant."

"You had no idea there was a threat," she said. "You carry no guilt for their deaths, Balien. You couldn't protect them if you didn't know."

Balien hugged her tighter. "How well you know me." He cleared his throat. "If I were there—"

"Then we might all be dead," she said. "We don't know how many there were. They might have known you were there. They might have sent a legion of Grigori. They might have overwhelmed you, and then Mother and Father and I would all be dead."

She felt the tension in his shoulders ease a little.

"You didn't know, Balien. No one knew."

"You are wise, my little librarian."

She pinched his arm, and it was the first time in months she'd felt like smiling. "I am not little."

"You are my delicate bird," he said gruffly. "Flying across the hills like… You know, maybe you are not a bird. Maybe you're my delicate goat."

She laughed, then slapped her hand over her mouth as Balien threw his leg over hers, trapping her beneath him.

"I love you so, Renata." He kissed her. "I *love* you. I would have nothing but joy for you, my love. Nothing but peace."

"You give me joy. You give me peace." She started humming a song to him, one of his favorites. It was the first song that had left her lips in months.

He closed his eyes. "I do not deserve you."

Renata felt her unused smile spread.

But that smile died when she heard whispers on the edge of her senses. They were a faint scratching sound, like claws on stone. She clutched Balien's nightshirt as her heart began to race.

"Renata?"

"They're here."

In seconds, the *talesm* that covered his body burst to life with magic.

"Be quiet." He sprang from bed, slipped on his boots, and reached for his weapons. "I'll get your father. Stay here."

His strength could not distract from the growing voices encroaching. Renata covered her ears and bit her lip so hard she tasted blood.

"There are too many," she whispered. "Too many. Too many. Too many."

Balien shook her shoulders. "Renata, how many?"

"I can't tell."

"How many?" he yelled.

"I can't— Too many!"

Dozens of clawing minds surrounded them. They were coming like an avalanche, surrounding the house. The useless magic she'd been taught died on her tongue. She was no warrior. As fierce as her mate was, this enemy was too much for him. Too much for her parents. They had been running too long.

She looked at Balien. "I love you. I promise I'll be brave."

"No!" he yelled, seeing the resignation in her eyes.

Renata heard the street door crack. She heard her father rushing down the stairs and her mother whispering spells in her bed. Renata saw the wheels turning in Balien's head a moment before he jumped on the bed, reached for his sword, and plunged it into the rafters. Punching with sheer force and rage, he tore open a hole in the old roof and dragged her up, shoving her through as she heard her father's soul go silent.

"Run!" he roared. "Renata, you must run!"

Her mother's voice was gone.

She shook her head. She heard the feet on the stairs. So many of them. Too many.

She couldn't leave him. She didn't want to live if he didn't.

"RENATA, YOU MUST RUN!"

SHE HAD NOTHING.

Nothing.

Renata hid in a human church for days, willing the Grigori to find her. But because heaven was perverse, they never did. Days passed. Then a week. She considered searching for the nearest scribe house, but Balien had known none of the brothers there. He didn't trust them. He only trusted those he knew, and he knew none of the scribes serving in Rome.

She left Rome, traveling north, hiding in churches at night.

It was winter and bitterly cold, but icy winds didn't bother her, so she had the roads to herself. When it began to rain, she found another church. Sometimes she thought she saw shadows in the trees and heard the distant soul voices of other Irin, but none of them approached her. She wore heavy clothing and sheared her hair when it became tangled. She didn't bathe. She only ate enough to survive.

Every night, she prayed to heaven that the Grigori would find her and give her peace.

They never did. *also out*

Renata traveled north. Venice was the only port she knew of, so she took the road to the sea, hoping to find a ship that could take her to the east. She had half her family's gold sewn in the hems of her garments, and she thought she had enough money to buy passage to Jaffa. Balien had spoken about a brother who lived there. Perhaps, if she made it to Jaffa, she could find Balien's people. She had the ring he'd given her, and his seal on her forehead. Perhaps it would be enough and they would give her some kind of home.

She had no one and nothing. *cut glass*

She was sleeping in a church outside Ravenna when she woke to a hand over her mouth. Renata's eyes went wide as something dragged her from the base of the altar and into the shadows of a chapel. Her heart raced for a second before she slumped against her attacker.

Finally.

She let out the breath she'd been holding for months, waiting for the cool piercing metal at the base of her spine that would release her from the hell she'd been living in.

The cold silver never came. The hand over her mouth eased away, and two dark brown hands turned her around. She blinked in the darkness, trying to see who was with her. No one spoke. In the dim candlelight, she could see a figure unwrapping the heavy scarves around their head. The face revealed was a woman's with skin darker than any Renata had seen. It was the color of seasoned walnut and perfectly smooth except for a vicious red wound on her cheek and jaw.

Whoever she was, her magic was strong. She was unquestionably Irina.

"Who are you?" Renata croaked out. It was the first time she'd used her voice in weeks.

The woman held up a finger and reached into a leather bag. She reached inside and brought out a leather roll. She unrolled the makeshift scroll, and a rag and chalk fell into her hand.

She carefully wrote in Latin: *I can't speak. My name is Mala. The Grigori took my voice.*

The woman unwound the cloth from around her throat, showing Renata the raw edges of a wound that looked like it had taken out most of her throat. The wound looked like it had been made by an animal's teeth. It was ragged, red, and swollen.

Renata reached for the chalk in the woman's hand, but the woman wrote again, *I can hear.*

"It's infected. Your wound is infected."

Mala shrugged.

"I can heal it for you."

Mala cocked her head as if to say, *Really?*

Renata realized too late what she had offered. She hadn't sung a song since Balien had died. She hadn't wanted to. But the woman was an Irina. She'd been wounded. Renata had a duty to help her.

Are you a healer? the Irina wrote on the leather, wiping out the words after Renata read them.

"No, I'm an archivist."

The woman's eyes gleamed with respect. An Irina archivist was like a walking magical library.

"I know the song, but it might not work as well as if a true healer sang it," Renata said. "What about you? Why are you here? Is your mate in Rome?"

Mala's eyes went cold. *They killed him while he was defending our scribe house. I came to this country to tell his mother, but she is dead too.*

"My whole family is dead, and my mate." Grief sat like icy air in her lungs, making it hard to breathe. "We weren't mated yet, but he was my *reshon.*"

The woman clasped both Renata's hands between her own, and Renata knew from the silent grief crying in her mind that Mala had also lost her soul mate.

"What do we do now?" Renata said. "Nowhere is safe. We traveled to Rome to escape, but they still found us. Most nights I just want death to find me, sister."

The woman's eyes turned fierce. She shook her head vehemently and wrote: *Not until we kill as many of them as they have killed.* She drew back her cloak, revealing the wicked curved blade at her waist. Renata had never seen a blade like that, but then she'd never seen an Irina like this woman.

"I don't know how to fight," Renata said. "I'm an archivist."

So? the woman wrote.

"No one ever taught me."

My mate taught me. He was a warrior. Many of the Irina in my clan are warriors.

Why hadn't Balien taught her to use a sword or fight? Why didn't she know any Irina warriors? Among her peers, they were only the subject of legends. Irina fought centuries ago, not in the more civilized modern age. Scribes were the ones who handled the dirty business of fighting off Grigori.

"And look where we are now," Renata murmured.

The woman tapped her knee. *What is your name?*

"Renata."

She eyed the fierce woman with the curved blade. She had calluses and scars on her hands, just like Balien and her father.

"Can you teach me?" Renata asked. "Can you teach me to be a warrior?"

The woman smiled a little. *Can you heal my wound?*

Renata held out her hand and Mala grasped it. "Deal."

CHAPTER TWO

Prague, 1999

Maxim lifted the beer and drank half of it before his companion sat down.

"You like the beer in Prague?" the scribe named Vilem said. "It's good, isn't it?"

"Best in Europe," Max said.

"And cheap." Vilem looked around the club in the basement off Old Town Square. Young people were everywhere and the music was pounding.

Max wasn't worried about paying for beer. The watcher who'd sent him on this intelligence-gathering mission had given him plenty of funds. Though he was technically assigned to the scribe house in Istanbul, Maxim traveled all over eastern Europe, trading favors, listening to rumors, and sharing beers with scribes like Vilem.

Vilem was technically a rogue, but he was a harmless one. Max could sympathize with not wanting to bow to a power structure. Once, it would have been nothing for an Irin scribe to make his own way in the world. As long as they didn't harm anyone, the Elder Council would leave scribes and singers to live their lives.

That was life before the Rending. Life after the Rending meant the Irin population was cut in half. Three out of every four Irina were gone, along with hundreds of scribes who had died trying to protect them. Their people, already scarce, were struggling to survive. The Irina who'd survived the Rending hid in havens around the world. Some scribes had never even seen a female of their own race.

The few scribes whose mates survived the Rending went with them into hiding, choosing to defy an increasingly controlling power structure in Vienna that had become paranoid and protective. Some of those families produced children like Vilem. Young. Mostly untrained. Powerful offspring of their half-angelic blood with none of the discipline the scribe houses wrought.

"Where are you from?" Max asked Vilem.

Vilem was silent.

"I'm not interested in turning you in to a watcher or exposing your family," Max said. "I'm simply trying to understand how you came across this information and why you're choosing to share it."

"Because it's not right," Vilem said. "It's just not right."

"What's not right?"

Vilem drank his beer in silence for a few more minutes, letting the dance music assault Max's ears until a headache threatened.

"I'm from Dresden."

Max nodded but didn't speak. Dresden fell in a territorial grey area. After the Forgiven angels had returned to the heavens, leaving their Irin children behind with their magic, the Fallen were the only true angels on earth. The problem was they were far from the peaceful creatures the humans imagined. The Fallen fought among themselves, breeding with human women to produce half-blood offspring called Grigori.

But though the Irin and Grigori shared angelic blood, they shared little else.

26

"What's the situation in Dresden?" Max asked. "The nearest scribe house is Berlin, is it not?"

"We live well," Vilem said. "It's not as bad as you might think."

"With no Irin guardians there in an official capacity?" Max asked. "No Grigori patrols? I would assume—"

"*Don't* assume." Vilem ran his hands through his hair, looking around the club nervously. "That's the problem. Everyone assumes because of the past. And I understand why, but it's not... It's just not what you think."

"Boy, what are you talking about?" Though Max wasn't quite two hundred years old, he was far more worldly than this young scribe whose *talesm* didn't even reach his collar.

"We don't need Irin protection," Vilem said.

"The whole world needs Irin protection," Max said. "Whether they know it or not."

Grigori seduced and fed from the souls of humanity, often leaving nothing in their wake but a shell of a person. Most often, they left a corpse. They had a particular liking for young female travelers. It was one of the reasons there were so many scribes in Prague.

And the Fallen? They reveled in the destruction their offspring wrought. Human were nothing to them. They staked out territory to play games and control riches; archangels were the worst of all.

Max finished his beer and caught the waitress's eye to ask for another. Vilem was nervous, tapping his finger on the table and glancing over his shoulder.

From what Max knew, two archangels, Svarog and Volund, were influential in Dresden, but neither truly held it. Because of that, numerous minor angels struggled for control, often killing each other in the process.

The most recently deceased angel—and his offspring—were the subject of Max's inquiries.

"You have to understand," Vilem said, "Cassius wasn't controlling. He let his children live their lives. He wasn't ambitious, so his sons... They have no reason to be aggressive. Do you understand?"

"They are Grigori."

"But they don't have to be violent."

Max's eyes narrowed. "How do you know this?"

The young man went pale, but he didn't look away. "I have a friend."

"What kind of friend?"

"A Grigori friend."

Max's arm shot across the booth as he grabbed Vilem by the throat. The waitress who was returning with his beer gasped and dropped the glass before she ran away.

"Please," Vilem choked out. "Please listen."

"We are not *friends* with Grigori," Maxim hissed. "They are demons. Monsters who raped and murdered our women. Who turned our children to dust. We are not friends with them. We hunt them like the animals they are."

Vilem tried to pry Maxim's hand loose. "Not... all..."

"The Grigori who participated in the Rending are mostly gone," said a smooth voice to Max's left.

Max let Vilem go and immediately reached for the silver dagger in the sheath at his shoulder.

The Grigori who'd spoken raised both hands. "I come in peace."

Which was a good thing. Max had been so angered by Vilem's words he'd completely lost awareness of his surroundings. If he'd been paying better attention, he would have noticed the telltale scent of sandalwood growing stronger. Max's eyes swept the room, looking for more, but the Grigori appeared to be alone. They were sitting in a corner, hidden by shadows as pulsing lights swirled around the dance floor.

Max didn't want to startle the humans, but he kept his hand on the handle of his dagger. "What is this?"

"Hopefully a conversation and not an execution," the Grigori said.

28

Max's eyes darted between a pale and frightened Vilem and the Grigori.

The man was, in all ways Max could see, exactly like others of his race. He was fine-featured and attractive. His scent designed to be alluring to the humans around him. Grigori were perfect predators. Once they touched a human, the man or woman would do nearly anything the Grigori wanted. Often, their victims wept and fought against being rescued.

But Grigori also had a nearly manic energy, a crackling kind of magic that careened out of control. They had all the power of angelic blood with none of the control.

Except for this man.

"What are you?" Max said. "You're not like the others."

"There are more of us than you might think." The man kept his hands in his pockets. "My name is Charles, and Cassius was my sire."

"Cassius is dead."

"He is," Charles said. "Which means that for the first time in my life, my brothers and I are truly free."

***

MAX LEFT THE BAR, following behind both Vilem and Charles, unwilling to let the Grigori out of his sight. He had to admit he was intrigued. Charles was unlike any Grigori Max had ever stalked. He exuded a concentrated focus. Max could see him resisting the advances of the human women who propositioned him. They were drawn to his scent and magic, intoxicated by it, but Charles ignored them. Max could see the effort, and it astonished him. It was the first time in his life he'd seen any Grigori exhibit control.

"You'll see," Vilem said. "You'll see when you meet Josef and the others."

"Others?" Max asked.

"I allowed Josef to bring two friends with him. None of them have been out of the compound before," Charles said. "They're very disciplined, but they need experience around humans if they're ever going to live anything close to a normal life."

"Is that your goal?" Max asked. "For them to live a normal life? What does that mean for Grigori?"

"For us?" Charles frowned. "It means not being monsters."

According to Charles, Grigori whose fathers were dead had free will and could be taught—*disciplined* was the word the Grigori used —to live peacefully. It was a struggle against their nature, but it was possible.

"Those like Josef and his friends are our hope," Charles said. "They were young when Cassius died. Young enough to have no memory of violence. Their identity has not yet been set. They were willing to live by my rules."

"What about your brothers who don't want to live by your rules?"

"They've fled Dresden," Charles said. "Or I killed them."

Charles and Vilem walked north toward the narrow streets of the Jewish Quarter. They passed a line of quiet restaurants in neat reconstructed buildings and turned right into a narrow residential complex that looked more empty than occupied. There was a small garden on the corner, and graffiti decorated a plywood fence propped against a broken wall. Prague was in a constant state of repair these days.

They entered the courtyard and headed for a set of heavy metal doors that looked like a holdover from the communist era. More graffiti. More plywood. Max went on alert the minute he ducked through the doorway.

Vilem was a lamb. Though Charles seemed legitimate in his manner, all this could be a trap. He brushed a thumb over his wrist, activating his *talesm*.

"I understand your caution," Charles said quietly. "But please trust me. I want peace with your people. That's all I'm looking for."

"So you say."

They climbed two flights of stairs, Max keeping them in his sights the whole way.

"You'll see," Charles said. "When you meet the young ones, you'll see. They're not like the others."

Charles went right when they reached the second floor and walked halfway down the hall. Max looked around and listened, but he didn't hear a sound. The complex appeared to be under construction. There were various tools parked in corners, and much of the ragged industrial carpet had been torn up. There were no human voices or scents at all. The whole building felt deserted.

The Grigori knocked twice on a door before he opened it. "Josef?"

There was no answer, and something cold slithered along the back of Max's neck. An unfamiliar energy lingered in the narrow entryway. He turned and saw a flash of dark hair disappear at the far end of the hallway.

A woman?

Charles walked farther into the flat. "Xavier? Paul?"

Max followed them, grim suspicion making his feet heavy.

Charles and Vilem stood in the middle of the living room where the remnants of a meal sat cooling on the coffee table. Charles was staring at the old sofa along the wall.

"I don't understand," Vilem said. "What's going on?"

Child.

Max knew what the crumbled clothes meant. He saw the remnants of dust on the sofa and the floor. There were no signs of struggle. Nothing appeared to be upended. That was the most disturbing part. The Grigori boys had been killed where they sat, not appearing to offer even token resistance to their deaths.

Charles lifted his eyes to Max. "How did you find them?"

Max shook his head. "I did not do this."

Rage and grief colored the Grigori's cheeks red. "Your people did this!"

Max glanced at Vilem and spoke calmly, trying to defuse the

situation before the Irin boy was harmed. "This was not a sanctioned killing, Charles. Think. I knew nothing of this place. How would I tell anyone about it?"

"Your people tracked them. They tracked them and—"

"You know what our mandate is."

"Kill Grigori!" Charles yelled. "Even if they're trying to live in peace. Even if they—"

"We protect humans," Max said. "Do we attack known sanctuaries? Only if humans are being kept inside. We only attack Grigori when they prey on humans. This was not sanctioned by any watcher, Charles. There aren't any girls here."

But there had been a woman.

Vilem said, "Wait. What are you saying?" He turned to the sofa and the empty clothes. "Are you saying—"

"Your friends are dead," Max said calmly. "But this was not ordered by a watcher."

"Says the scribe who's a lapdog for the corrupt council in Vienna," Vilem said, inching behind Charles.

"Vilem, come with me." Max held out his hand, worried about the Grigori. Charles seemed calm, but would the loss of his brothers send him into a murderous rage? "Boy, come with me now."

"No." Vilem eyes shone, but his mouth was firm. "Charles is my friend. Josef was my friend. They helped my family when we couldn't trust the scribes. I'm not going anywhere with you."

At Vilem's words, the Grigori's rage crumbled. He knelt at the sofa, gathering the empty clothing of his brothers into his arms.

A mean, vengeful voice whispered inside Max's head: *now you know how it feels.*

He was a baby during the Rending, but he'd heard the stories. Whole families—whole villages—wiped out. Women and children killed in their beds.

He spoke to Vilem again. "I can help your family."

"We don't need your help." Tears were falling down Vilem's

cheeks. "Leave. Let us mourn in peace. Go hunt Grigori who are actual threats."

Max debated for a few silent minutes, but it was clear where the boy's loyalties lay.

"Fine," he said. "You have my number. You may call me anytime."

"I don't need you." The boy knelt by Charles. "We don't need any of you."

Max backed out of the room, listening for any movement in the hall. Someone had been here, and it hadn't been a scribe. It hadn't been anyone associated with a watcher. This looked nothing like an orderly hunt. This was a stealth attack that had rendered the boys immobile as they were being killed, and no scribe had magic like that.

He'd only taken three steps out of the building when he felt the point of a knife at his spine.

"Tell me," a soft voice said, "what business a scribe has with monsters?"

It was the woman he'd seen. It had to be.

"You killed the boys." Max tried to turn, but the blade pressed harder.

"I killed three little monsters who had lured two human girls into their den."

Max closed his eyes. "I didn't see any girls."

"Of course not. They ran away when the boys fell asleep so suddenly. Very strange, the girls said. Were the boys drunk?"

"Who are you?" he asked.

"You don't need to know that."

"You don't want to touch me," he said. "I could hurt you."

She might have been armed, but Max's touch could have the same effect as the Grigori. Irin scribes weren't allowed to touch human women. Their souls held the same hunger as the Grigori; they just had the magic to control it.

"I know what you are, scribe."

Who was she?

Max didn't like being helpless. He didn't like being threatened. And he was running out of patience. Before the knife could press closer, he ducked to the left and spun around, grabbing the arm that held the knife. Instead of bare skin, he met a long leather glove. Smiling, Max wrenched her wrist, causing her to drop the knife, then he spun her around, reversing their positions so he held her in a headlock. The woman didn't flinch. She whispered something under her breath, and Max's arms turned to dead weight. Then she stomped on his instep and kicked up with the heel of her shoe, nearly hitting his groin. He twisted to the side to avoid the blow, only to lose his grip on her.

She dove for her knife and crouched across from him in a fighting stance.

Max's eyes went wide. "Who are you?"

"What's wrong?" Her tone was taunting. "Don't you know any girls who fight?"

She smiled and Max noticed how beautiful she was. She wasn't just beautiful, she was stunning. Long reddish-brown hair and eyes so deep he could fall into them. She was nearly as tall as he was and built lean and long. Long legs. Rounded hips.

Her full lips parted, and she whispered more words. Words in the Old Language.

Her magic brought Max to his knees, and he went willingly, lifting astonished eyes to her precious face. "Irina." His heart ached saying the word. "You're Irina."

***

"You need to stop staring," she said, sitting across from him in the cozy basement pub across the Charles Bridge.

She was digging into a bowl of goulash and not eating delicately. She tore off hunks of brown bread as if she hadn't eaten in days. Her weapons glinted from under her long brown overcoat, stored in shoulder holsters very like his own.

"I can't," Max said.

"Have you *never* met an Irina before? Not once?"

"I saw one once in Vienna, but only at a distance. I went to the library to deliver a report, and I saw her in the gallery. She was covered though." He passed a hand over his face. "She didn't want anyone to see her face."

The Irina's eyes turned inward. "Just one?"

Max nodded.

"And the Elder singers' desks?"

"The Elder singers' desks have been vacant for two hundred years," he said. "I've only heard stories about their songs."

Her jaw tensed. "So we are only rumors now."

"Legends. Stories. Myths."

"I'm not a myth." She started eating again. "Do I look like a myth?"

"You look like a dream," Max said.

She rolled her eyes. "How old are you?"

"Nearly two hundred years."

She went silent.

"Tell me your name," Max said. "My name is Maxim of Riga. I was born—"

"I don't need to know anything about you," the woman said. "And you don't need to know my name."

"Why?" He'd beg if she asked. She was the most beautiful—the most hopeful—thing Max had ever seen. "Are the Irina returning?"

"We never left."

"You did," he whispered. "I had no mother. No aunts. No sisters. I've never even felt an Irina's touch. How can you say you never left?"

She looked up. "You've never felt an Irina's touch?"

Max's cheeks flushed. "Of course I haven't."

She looked him up and down, her eyes wide. "So you've never—"

"That's none of your business." He grew irritated with her stubbornness. "Contact with human women is not sanctioned by the Watchers' Council. It's too dangerous."

Not that he'd been wholly obedient. Max gave lip service to the Watchers' Council, but he was far from a model scribe. Much could be accomplished with a willing woman and a pair of gloves.

"The Watchers' Council," she muttered. "Mandating even the sex lives of their scribes since 1810."

"Someone must have control," Max said. "Or we will turn into the monsters we hunt. We no longer have our Irina."

"We were never *yours*." Her eyes flashed. "Your council forgot that, didn't they?"

"At least they didn't run."

She pounded a fist on the table. "Don't lecture me about running."

He leaned forward, unafraid of her anger. "What is your name?"

"Why do you need to know?"

"Because..." He didn't have a reason. "I just need to know. I won't tell anyone about seeing you. I will vow it on my mother's name, if you wish. I won't tell anyone you killed those boys."

"Those boys had two human girls in that room with them," she said. "I don't know why you thought they were innocents, because I saw them. They were looking at those girls as if they were dinner and the girls were more than happy to go along with it. I saved their lives."

"I believe you."

"Who was that Grigori with you? Why were you talking to him?"

"He claimed to be living a peaceful life," Max said. "He said it's possible to live without violence if the angel who fathered you is dead."

"You don't seem like a fool. You don't believe him, do you?"

"I haven't decided yet," Max said. "The older Grigori *was* different. As for the younger men, I suspect that fresh temptation was too much to resist, no matter what their training. Their brother said they hadn't been around human women before, and when that level of temptation exists…"

Max stared at the hand that rested on the table. Her fingers were long and delicate, but there were calluses there. She fought with the staff and the dagger. A lethal female of his own race. Could there be anything more tempting? Max's confusion over the events of the evening was quickly being overtaken by fascination for the woman before him.

She saw him staring. Slowly she turned her palm up.

Max's heart beat faster. He reached out a hand but drew it back and planted it palm down on the table.

"Go ahead," she said softly.

"Are you sure?"

She reached over and grabbed his hand, knitting their fingers together a second before the sheer energy of her magic punched through Max.

He gasped and held on tightly. "Heaven above."

"I haven't touched one of the brothers at our compound in some time," she said softly. "This helps me too."

Because Irina channeled the soul voices of the world, they needed contact with Irin to leach off energy. Irin males absorbed it, making themselves stronger and steadier. Touching this Irina was like being hit with a punch of magic that warmed Max from the inside out.

He lifted her hand and pressed her palm to his cheek, closing his eyes as he leaned into her touch.

"Tell me your name," he whispered. "Please."

"Renata. My name is Renata." Her pulse pounded against his cheek. "What are you doing?"

Heaven above, he was kissing her wrist. The need had been instinctive. Max pulled back but kept his hand over hers, still pressing it to his cheek, afraid she'd take away the life and heat he'd given her. "I'm sorry."

"Don't be." Her eyes were wary, but her lips were flushed. Renata's thumb reached over and brushed over Max's lips, making him shudder. "This is the first touch you've felt," she said softly.

Skin to skin? Irin to Irina? Max nodded.

"What do you see when you look at me, Maxim of Riga?"

"You're beautiful," Max said. "The most beautiful thing I've ever seen. You're powerful. Dangerous."

"Does that threaten you?"

"No. It turns me the fuck on," he muttered.

Her pulse beat faster and her eyes locked on his lips. She was vital and alive and wanted him as much as he wanted her. He saw it in her eyes.

He asked, "When was the last time—"

"None of your business."

Too long. That was what her heartbeat was saying. She hadn't once tried to pull away from his touch.

Max slid out of the booth, keeping hold of Renata's hand. He reached in his pocket and left far too much money on the table before he pulled Renata out the door and up the dark stairs. When they reached the top, he turned into a quiet alleyway and pushed her against the wall of the inn, grasping her hips and squeezing as he brought his mouth down to hers.

His lips hovered over hers. "I've never kissed before." Kissing without skin contact was pointless.

Renata smiled. "I'll be gentle." She brushed her lips over his. Once. Twice.

"That's enough of that," Max muttered. He angled his head and sank his teeth into her full lower lip.

Renata gasped, then took his mouth in a ravenous kiss that matched the hunger he felt.

There you are.

Max lifted her against the wall, and Renata wrapped her long legs around his hips, pulling him closer. Her arms went around his shoulders, and the hair on the nape of his neck rose at her touch. The hilts of her silver blades dug into his chest, and Max's *talesm* came alive, glowing silver in the darkness.

There you are.

CHAPTER THREE

Bergen, Norway
2005

R enata paused in the hallway outside her flat; the distinctive scent and magic she sensed was unmistakable.

Fucking Maxim.

She turned the knob and walked into the apartment, dropping her bag by the front door.

Max was stretched on the futon, his long legs hanging over the end. His arms were folded behind his head and he was grinning.

She wanted to slap him. And sink her teeth into his bicep. This was not an uncommon reaction to Max.

"What are you doing here?"

"How was your trip, darling?" His smug smile never wavered.

"How did you find this place?" She took off her coat and very pointedly did not remove her weapons.

Max swung his legs over the edge and stood in one smooth movement. He was astonishingly graceful for a large man, and it drove her crazy to watch him move. Watching him fight was even more of a turn-on. He knew it and he used it.

Which also drove her crazy.

"You told me I'd never find your home," he said. "You can't say things like that and not expect me to search for you."

Her secrets were not only about pride. The haven where her community of sisters lived was not that far away. Yes, it was hidden in a valley farther north and guarded by old and powerful magic, but even being in the same country felt too close. Too intrusive. Not unlike Max.

"This thing we have," she said quietly. "It is not a relationship."

"The hell it isn't." His smile died. "You can tell yourself that if it makes you feel better, but we both know the truth."

"It's *not* a relationship," she said. "And it'll stop being anything at all unless you back off."

His eyes flashed. "I can see you didn't kill quite enough Grigori on this hunting trip. Need to burn off some energy?"

"Fuck off." She unstrapped her weapons and hung them in the entryway before she locked the deadbolts on her door and set the alarm. How the hell had he broken in? She'd stopped trying to figure out how Max did anything a few years before. He had skills and contacts she didn't know about, and she refused to ask. Asking only made whatever this was feel more real. More intimate. More permanent.

It wasn't. Her *reshon* was dead. She wasn't looking for a mate. Max could never compare to Balien.

But Renata knew part of her anger stemmed from the gratitude she felt seeing him. She was tired. Worn out. And part of her was happy to not walk into an empty flat. She wasn't going to tell him that.

She slept with Max because he was a skilled lover, and Renata knew both of them needed some level of connection. She even considered him a friend. But that was all. That was all it was ever going to be.

She went to the kitchen and filled the electric kettle. She'd flown into Bergen from Aberdeen and hadn't even bothered to get her car from long-term parking. She was too tired. She'd taken a cab to her apartment and spent most of the short drive home thinking about her bed.

And possibly thinking about a strong pair of arms to hold her, but the last she'd heard, Max had been in Istanbul.

She didn't go there. He wasn't supposed to come here. Those were the rules, and he'd broken them.

Renata felt him come into the kitchen. Max's energy was unmistakable, and her betraying body responded. She braced her hand on the counter when he came behind her. Without a word, he brushed her long hair away from her neck and started kissing her. She angled her head to the side and let the tension and manic energy drain from her body into his. He licked and scraped his teeth against her skin, sucking on the spot that sent her pulse racing. His arms came around her, one heavy hand palming her breast as the other went low on her belly and pressed her body into his. She felt his arousal as he unbuckled her belt.

"Let me," he whispered. "You need it."

She nodded wordlessly, and his hand slid beneath her panties. She gasped and clutched the edge of the counter when his fingers found her wet and swollen.

"Fast now." He bit her neck and squeezed her breast. "Slow later."

"Yes."

He brought her to mind-shattering orgasm before the kettle boiled.

Max turned Renata around when she could barely stand. His kiss was long and lazy. "Go lie down," he said. "Get out of those clothes, and I'll make the tea."

She nodded and did what he said. If she was less exhausted, she'd be more angry at his high-handed orders, but she simply didn't have it in her. She was emotionally and physically wrung out.

She went to the bedroom and shut the heavy drapes, dropping

her clothes on the floor before she tumbled into bed and let her eyes close.

Safe. When Max was with her, she knew she'd be able to sleep. Knew that if the monsters came knocking, he could kill them even faster than she could.

She didn't tell him that either.

A few minutes later, he brought a cup of tea in and set it on the bedside table. He stripped off his shirt and pants. His boxers were tossed on top of her clothes. Then he drew back the sheet and slid into bed beside her.

"Come here," Max said, hooking her leg over his hip. He was already hard when he kissed her. She could feel the length of him pressing against her. She was half-asleep, but she wanted him. She wanted to fall asleep with his weight on her.

"Fuck me," she murmured, guiding him into her body. She let out a groan of relief when his hips bucked against hers. He was seated to the hilt, his muscled arms caging her in, his massive shoulders blocking everything from her sight except him. Only Max.

"I'm not fucking you," he whispered in her ear. He moved in steady rhythm, and his weight pressed her into the bed. "That's not what this is."

She didn't argue. He was going to make her come again. She hovered on the edge.

"You know what this is," Max said. "You know what we are."

She cried out when she orgasmed and let the tears come when he finally groaned his own release and lowered himself beside her. She wrapped her arm around his shoulders and didn't say a word when he tucked his face into her neck. Max's arm fell over her torso, and he let out a long breath.

"Sleep," he whispered. "We'll talk in the morning."

They wouldn't. She couldn't bring herself to end it even though she knew she should. No matter how many Grigori she killed, she still felt dead inside. She was hollow, and she needed him too much.

Cardiff, Wales
2010

SHE PICKED up her phone on the second ring, but all she heard was silence.

"Max?"

There was nothing but ragged breath on the other end of the line.

"Max, what's wrong?" Renata stood, leaving the table where a map of the city was spread out. She ignored the confused stares of her companions. She was working on a job with two Irina from North Wales, hoping to exterminate a nest of Grigori that was running a hostel in the mountains where young women were going missing.

She walked out of the room and up the stairs of the narrow house they'd rented. "I'm alone. What's going on? Where are you?"

"I'm not hurt." His voice was rough. "I just... I needed to hear your voice."

"Where are you?"

"It's not important," he whispered. "Are you safe?"

Renata took a deep breath. "You have to stop asking that."

It had become a bad habit in the past couple of years. Max never used to ask her about her jobs. She'd tell him or she wouldn't. He didn't ask what she was doing or where she was going. A few times a year, one of them would text the other. When they needed to, they would meet. That was all that was allowed. Sometimes they went over a year without seeing each other, though that was more Renata's stubbornness than anything Max wanted.

"I know how to take care of myself," Renata said. "You know that."

"I just lost a friend." His voice was hard. "Indulge me."

Her senses went on alert. "Where are you?"

"Oslo. Are you in Bergen?"

Damn. "No, I'm in the UK."

"Where?"

She thought about the Irina downstairs. If she brought a scribe in, they'd leave her without a backward glance. "I can't tell you that."

"Damn it, Reni. All I want—"

"I'm in the middle of something," she said. "I'm with good people. Competent people. That's all I can give you."

"You're never willing to give me much, are you?" His voice was bitter. "I suppose I should be used to that by now."

She'd be angry, but his grief was too raw. "Is Leo with you?" He'd told her about his family, even when she tried to ignore him. It was too much intimacy, but Max told her anyway. "Is Malachi? Rhys?" A tremor of alarm. "Are your brothers all right?"

"It wasn't one of my brothers," Max said, his voice going dead again. "It was a friend. I should let you go. You're busy."

"Max, I'm—"

He hung up.

"Sorry," she whispered. *I'm sorry.*

Vienna, Austria
2014

SOMEONE WAS POUNDING on the door of the rented flat, and she knew it could only be Max. He'd left his key with her. She went to open the door and backed out of his way as he stormed in.

"'I'll see you when I see you?'" he shouted. "What was that, Renata?"

She closed her eyes and let his anger smash and fall against the hard wall she'd erected. Then she walked back to the bedroom and continued packing her things.

She'd been in Vienna too long.

The Battle of Vienna would be one to write songs about. If she were still an archivist, she'd already be composing one. The battle of the four archangels, two of them sacrificing themselves in a grand attempt at redemption while giving the Irin and Irina warriors time to fight back the army of Grigori that flooded the city, joined by their new allies, the free Grigori and their newly discovered sisters.

It would be a beautiful and frightening song. Threaded between the grand battles, Renata could sing a softer harmony of quiet nights and peaceful mornings spent with the scribe currently storming through the apartment.

Max stood in the doorway of the bedroom they'd shared, glaring at her and the suitcase on the bed.

"This is it?" he asked her. "This is what you're doing?"

"What did you expect me to do?" she asked. "Run away to Istanbul with you? Leave my life behind?"

"Everything has changed!" he shouted. "The Irina have come back. The singers' council has reformed. You don't have to hide anymore."

Her mouth fell open. "You did. You expected me to abandon my sisters and run away to be your little mate."

Max grabbed her shoulders. "Would that be so awful? To be my mate? To have a life with me?"

She wrenched herself away from him. "You know *nothing*."

"You're right." He slammed the bedroom door shut. "Because you refuse to tell me. It's been fifteen years, Renata. I don't even know where you were born. I don't know who your parents were. I don't know what your training was. I don't know anything about your life before every damn thing in our world went to shit."

She ignored him and went back to packing.

"Who was your mother?" He stood behind her, looking over her shoulder. "What was her name? I've told you everything, and you tell me nothing. Who was your father? What is the mark on your forehead? Does it have something to do with who you were?"

"You want to know who I was?" She slammed her suitcase and spun around, shoving him back.

"Yes!"

"I was a fool!" she shouted. "I was a little girl who sang songs about history and magic and thought they meant something. I was a weakling who thought that a mountain and the warrior I loved could protect me from anything."

She saw his eyes narrow.

"Did you think there was only you, Maxim?" She pointed to her forehead where Balien's mark still shone when her magic was high. "I was supposed to be mated. That's what this mark is."

There. She saw the hurt in his eyes. *Is that enough knowledge for you?*

"You know what?" he said through gritted teeth. "I don't care. You're lying to yourself if you say we don't have a relationship. We're good together, Renata. Hell, we have the exact same job. There's no reason we shouldn't work together. We make the perfect team."

He was right. And she couldn't do it. She couldn't do it to him. Deep in her gut, she knew that one day Max would find his *reshon* and it wouldn't be her. He'd find the woman heaven had created for him and it would be perfect harmony. He deserved that. He deserved more than a half-dead woman whose heart had been ripped from her chest.

For months she'd used the excuse of them working together to indulge herself. She'd slept next to him at night, fought by his side, laughed and eaten meals with him, pretending that what they had could be something more.

How could she say goodbye?

She felt the tears in her eyes and hated them. Hated her weakness.

Max came to her and grabbed her by the shoulders. "Just tell me why. I'm tired of this, Reni. I'm done pretending it's enough. I want more. I want a life together. I'd never leave you in Istanbul. Why would I? I want you to fight beside me. I love—"

"Don't tell me you love me," she said, squeezing her eyes shut. "You don't know what love is."

His hands dropped as if she'd burned them.

"The warrior I almost mated? His name was Balien of Damascus. He was a great man. A warrior who fought in the Crusades. He was a knight of Jerusalem, a Rafaene scribe, and my *reshon*. We knew the moment we saw each other, and his voice...?" She wiped away the tears that poured down her cheeks. "He was the other half of my soul. Loving him was the most beautiful thing in my life, and no other joy has ever compared to it. He gave his life saving mine."

Max was like a statue. She couldn't meet his eyes. She felt nothing from him. No anger. No pain. She kept her shields clamped shut, afraid to hear the voice of his soul.

"You're going to find that joy someday," she whispered. "And you deserve to. You're going to find your *reshon*, Maxim. Find your true mate." She took a deep breath and cut the last delicate ties holding them together. "But it's not going to be me. You're right. We should stop pretending."

By the time Renata looked up, all she could see was his back as Max walked out the door.

CHAPTER FOUR

Ciasa Fatima, 2017

Max stroked his fingers through Renata's hair, glancing at the dying embers of the fire as a cold morning sun breached the windows. It had snowed during the night, and only a sliver of daylight remained visible on the first floor. He'd have to get up and stoke the fire, but not until she woke. Renata lay against him, her body a warm and welcome weight against his chest. His arm was numb and he didn't care. She was sleeping in his arms, which meant he could stare at her. He hadn't had the privilege in nearly three years.

Renata let out a sigh as her eyes fluttered open.

"Good morning," he whispered.

She frowned for a second before she closed her eyes again and rolled to face the fire.

"It wasn't a dream," she muttered.

"Were you hoping it was?" Max asked. "I have to tell you, in my dreams, we're usually wearing less clothes."

"You need to leave today."

He pulled her back to his chest. "There's probably six feet of new snow out there. I'm not going anywhere. Neither are you. It's a good thing you've stored food in the kitchen."

She said nothing.

"Hey, Reni?" He kissed the top of her head. "How long has it been since we've seen each other?"

"Two years and ten months."

He smiled. *And four days.* "Do you know something?"

"I know lots of things," she said.

"It's been two years, ten months, and four days since you left me."

"You left me."

"You were packing your bags when I walked out the door, and you weren't there when I got back." He was getting off track. "That was two years, ten months, and four days ago."

"And?"

"I still haven't met my *reshon.*"

She shoved his arm from around her waist and stood.

"What?" He watched her reach for her robe and wrap it around herself like armor. "I just thought I'd let you know."

"Do you think you're funny?"

"No, I don't think I'm funny," he said. "I think I'm pissed off."

"Then why did you come?"

He let out a long breath. Why *had* he come?

"I told myself when I was walking up here—when I thought my toes might fall off from the cold—I didn't know if I was trying to find you for wanting or sheer obstinacy."

Renata was standing at the window, staring out into the blue wall of snow.

That's right. You're not getting rid of me so easily this time.

He looked around at the carved rafters and expertly stacked stone hearth. The house was plain from the outside but stunning within. "How old is this place?"

"The house?" Renata walked away from the window and sat in a wooden rocking chair by the hearth. "I don't know. It was here when I was born, so at least three hundred years, but it's been rebuilt over the years. Things were added on here and there. There are eight bedrooms upstairs, so you're welcome to prepare one for yourself if you like. Mine and the living room are the warmest though, so if I were you, I'd continue sleeping down here."

He'd be sleeping in her bedroom, but that discussion could wait. "This was your family's home?"

She shook her head, but she still wasn't looking at him. "It didn't belong to us. Not exactly. I'm sure the council has forgotten about it at this point. I've made sure the name on the deed is mine. They can't take it now." She turned. "I'm sure you're thinking they wouldn't be interested in a house this remote, but it's not the house they'd want. It's the caves."

Max sat up and leaned against the sofa. "I wondered if there were caves when I saw how the house was built."

"The caves are the only reason this house—this whole compound—ever existed. I don't know how old they are, but my mother told me they were created by very powerful earth singers centuries ago."

"Why?"

"To store the scrolls."

Understanding dawned. "This was a library."

Renata stood and grabbed wood for the fire, placing it on the glowing embers along with some kindling. "This was a library. A unique library. Ciasa Fatima was one of the few combined libraries in the world."

Max didn't say anything. For the first time since he'd known her, Renata was willingly sharing her past. It was as if she'd opened a jewel box and handed him rubies. He didn't want to say anything that might make her clam up.

"My mother came first. She apprenticed with the oldest singer in the mountains, the archivist here for hundreds of years. My father was a visiting scribe studying the history of Ariel's children in Europe. He came here, met my mother, and never left."

She fell silent, watching the fire light and grow.

"Did you have any siblings?" Max asked.

"No. Neither did my parents. It was just the three of us." She looked around the living room. "But it was never just the three of us, you know?"

He didn't know. Max hadn't been raised in any kind of home. He'd been surrounded by warriors and hard men his entire life. The first time he'd lived in anything that resembled a home was when his brother Malachi had brought his new mate, Ava, to the scribe house in Istanbul. That was only a few years before.

"Eight bedrooms," Max said. "There must have been many visitors."

She nodded. "It was the way of libraries in the old days. People were always moving in and out. A scribe and his family would come to study for a few years, then move on. A singer and her mate would visit for a few months. A few families, like mine, were based here and rarely left. My father insisted there always be at least one room open to shelter someone new, which is why so many bedrooms were added over the years. There are even caves in the library that were added for Rafaene scribes who were on respite."

The picture she painted was of a haven, a safe and peaceful place of learning and hospitality. Max could guess what had happened when the Rending reached them.

"So there were only academics here when it happened," he said quietly. Where had her warrior *reshon* been?

Renata was still staring at the fire. "Do you want to see the caves?"

"Am I a scribe?"

Renata let the edge of a smile touch her lips. "I don't know. I don't think I've ever seen you with books."

"I adore them." His love for the written word was surpassed only by his love for those in his very small family. "I simply don't get the opportunity to indulge very often the way I travel."

She stood. "Wrap up. There are wool things in the closet down the hall. Most people aren't prepared for how cold it gets at night, so I always keep extra wraps. The caves will be chilly."

He nodded and watched her walk up the stairs to her bedroom. His eyes were caught by the sunlight glinting on the fresh snow. Unless it stormed again, he estimated three days before the trail was passable. Renata was as stubborn a woman as heaven had ever created.

Max had three days to change her mind.

THE LARGE LIVING area narrowed to a hallway that led to several locked rooms, a cozy music room with instruments hanging on the walls—including a finely carved guitar Max itched to play—and the downstairs washroom. As promised, there was running water, but the taps were cold. He'd have to boil water for a bath later. Renata led him past the wood-paneled hallway and beyond a heavy oak door.

"The renters don't get access to the caves," she said.

"Do they ask?"

"Most don't. If they do, the manager tells them it's storage."

An ancient iron lock hung on the door. Renata unlocked it and pulled the door open. Max could feel the temperature drop the moment they stepped through. His breath frosted in the air as Renata shut the heavy door and handed him a lamp. He lit it and held it high. There were torches affixed to the walls. Renata walked to them and whispered something. One by one, the torches lit and a smooth passageway of polished rock was revealed.

"It gets warmer once you go deeper into the mountain," Renata said as they walked. "There are thermal springs. If I keep the door open, the house will heat this hallway, but it seems like a waste of energy most of the time."

Max ran his hands across the polished limestone in the tunnel. "Are there any scrolls left?"

"No. There is still magic in the caves though. The spells carved on the rocks weren't defaced. They were cut too deeply. I doubt the Grigori knew what they were to begin with."

As they walked, Max began to see the magic scribes had cut into the rock. Like the ritual room in Istanbul, the carved words in the Old Language were familiar, though the style of the writing was not. Max recognized spells meant to protect the caves and the knowledge within. Saw other, more practical spells, to ward off humidity, cold, and ice. He felt the passage grow warmer, but the air remained fresh and dry.

"Ventilation?" he asked.

"Extensive," Renata answered. "The caves probably took centuries to perfect. Even today, if you wanted to live in them, they wouldn't be uncomfortable. Chilly, but not freezing. The Irina builders used the air from the thermal springs to heat the rooms but allowed enough ventilation that the library never became too damp."

"Amazing."

"Yes." She opened another heavy door, this one wasn't locked, and lifted her lamp high. Then Renata walked to the center of the room, took a box of matches from her pocket, and lit a central hearth. Within seconds, the fire and a series of mirrors along the walls lit the room with a warm gold glow.

Max turned, taking it all in. It was a round cave with deep alcoves cut to hold scrolls and for storage. Wooden bookshelves had been made to line the walls, but they lay empty save for a few volumes that looked more human-made than Irin. Heavy wooden scribe tables sat empty, their inkwells long dry. A light coating of dust marked the benches and chairs. A well-worn sofa and reading chairs sat near the hearth.

"Who keeps it?" Max asked. The room was deserted, but it wasn't a wreck.

"Me." She walked around the room. "We didn't have time right after, but eventually Mala and I came back here and she helped me. I burned most everything that was left."

Max tried to imagine what it must have been like, clearing out the wreckage of a home and the remains of her dead community. Though their dead turned to dust, Irin still bled. There would have been blood and empty clothing. Furniture would have been wrecked and broken. Food left to spoil. Animal remains. She had cleared out the wreckage of a destroyed home with the help of a single friend. Max would have to remember to kiss Mala in gratitude the next time he saw her. She'd probably stab him, but that was fine.

Renata walked back to an arched hallway, taking her lamp with her. Max followed her as she pointed out different rooms. Storage. Humble sleeping quarters for Rafaene scribes. A playroom for the children. A ritual room where the sacred fire would have been tended before it had been snuffed out by violence.

"The caves were probably where the first Irin lived," Renata said. "Long before the house was built. Look at this." She entered a large alcove with intricately carved designs decorating it and turned to face Max with a smile. "Go back to the reading room."

He raised an eyebrow but turned and did what she said.

When he arrived, he turned. "I'm here!" he shouted.

"Can you hear me?" Her voice was soft. She hadn't shouted, but the sound had carried to every corner of the reading room.

"I can." He spun around the room with a smile. It was as if the sound of her voice surrounded him. "What is it? Speaking tubes?"

"Acoustics," Renata said, still at the end of the hallway. "When we—when my mother would sing a history, she would stand here so everyone could hear her. The acoustics of the hall carried it. The angles of the reading room magnified it. When my mother sang, she didn't sound like a single voice. She sounded like a chorus."

Max sat on the edge of the table. "Sing to me," he whispered.

"What?"

He walked back toward her. "That must have been incredible."

"It was." She stepped out of the alcove and turned right, stopping dead in her tracks as the hallway branched.

"What is it?"

She held up a lamp. "This is the hallway where the classrooms were."

"Let's look." Max took her hand and lifted his lamp, intrigued by a scent he'd caught in the air coming from the hallway.

Renata didn't move.

"Reni?"

"This is where the children ran," she said. "We found their clothes in the room at the end of this hall. There were six children here when they came. Four girls and two boys."

He didn't try to make her move. "And they ran to their classroom."

She nodded.

Max didn't wait for permission. He enfolded Renata in his arms and held her tight. She was frozen, but he kept holding her.

"Did you ever let yourself grieve?" he whispered.

"There wasn't time to grieve."

"There hasn't been time in two hundred years?"

"It's useless," she said, pulling away from his arms. "After a while… it's useless."

No, it wasn't, but it would take time for her to see that. Max was starting to understand Renata's walls. She'd never really allowed herself any kind of family after losing this one. She'd become part of the Irina community in exile, but only peripherally. She had a few friends—a very few—but she didn't live with them. She worked constantly, rarely staying in one place, even her own flat, more than a month.

"Our time in Vienna," he asked quietly, "was that the first time?"

She frowned. "What?"

"Was that the first time since the Rending that you'd shared a home with someone?"

She stiffened and tried to walk past him. "That wasn't a home. It was a rented flat we shared while we were working."

He caught her arm. "We slept in the same bed at night. We cooked and ate together. We hung our laundry and bitched about who needed to clean the bathroom. We laughed and fell asleep in front of the television."

"That isn't—"

"It was a home. Our home. Or at least the beginnings of one."

Renata said nothing. She didn't even look at him.

"You keep coming back here, don't you? Every Midwinter, you come. You keep looking for the same feeling you lost, but you won't find it because it was never the building. It wasn't these caves, even with all the history and love and magic I can feel lingering here."

He drew her closer, linking their hands together. Renata's face was blank, but she wasn't running away. Not yet.

Max lifted her hand to his mouth and kissed it. "Home is what we could have together, but you're too afraid to build it."

She wrenched her hand out of his grasp and left him in the tunnel.

Max let her go.

HE EXPLORED every nook and cranny of the library, studying the intricate carvings along the wall and the lists of singers and scribes whose names were carved into the walls. Next to the alcove was a list of the chief Irina archivists, ending with the name *Heidi von Meren*. In the reading room, the list of librarians ended with the name *Giorgio di Lanzo*. Were they Renata's parents? Max guessed they were, but there was no way to be certain. If the Rending hadn't happened, would Renata's name have followed Heidi's?

I was a little girl who sang songs about history and magic and thought they meant something.

57

Renata had been an archivist like her mother. She'd spent her whole life learning about Irin history and magic and could likely recite massive volumes of Irina history purely from memory. Prior to the Rending, she would have been a powerful and influential woman, valued anywhere in the Irin world for her magical skill and knowledge. Archivists were the kind of Irina who occupied the elders' seats in Vienna. They were influential and feared.

But Renata lived in hiding, venting her rage on the Grigori who had stolen her life.

Stolen her love.

His name was Balien of Damascus. He was a great man. A warrior... a knight of Jerusalem, a Rafaene scribe, and my reshon.

Who was Balien of Damascus, and why hadn't he protected this library? An Irin warrior with extensive training could fight off a dozen armed Grigori and not sustain injury. And why hadn't he mated with Renata as soon as he knew she was his *reshon*? The only mark she wore was a single sign on her forehead.

If Renata wanted to be his mate, Max would abandon his own brothers to claim her.

He returned to the passageway leading to the classrooms where the children had fled. In the last classroom on the left, he found where they must have died. Max set his lamp in front of the longest wall and sat on a bench carved into the rock, staring at a lush scene painted on the limestone.

Mala.

Max remembered his cousin mentioning that the fearsome warrior was also an artist, but he'd never seen her work. Despite the darkness in the caves, the scene glowed with vivid joy. Children of every color and age ran toward a golden mountain, surrounded by animals. Elephants and lions guarded their path as birds sang in the trees overhead. Monkeys clutched flowers and ate vibrant purple fruit. Sheep and antelope lay sleeping at the feet of the lions while cattle grazed on the hills in the distance.

It was a scene of paradise and joy. Laughter instead of tears. A scene designed for loved ones to stop and linger and remember beauty. Renata, frozen in grief, had probably never seen it.

But someone had. Because in this room—and several of the others—there wasn't a spot of dust on the table, and the lamp held a fresh beeswax candle. Childish drawings sat on a low school desk, and the smell of fresh bread lingered in the air.

Someone was living in the caves, and judging by the smell of bread, they hadn't been gone long.

CHAPTER FIVE

id you ever let yourself grieve?

What a ridiculous question. Renata knocked back the dough she'd set out to rise the night before, kneading it a touch more before she began to shape the loaf. In the chilly air, it took a full day to bake her mother's honeyed bread, but it was the only thing to do at Midwinter. She'd already chopped the dried fruit and nuts she'd sprinkle on top. She split the dough into three ropes, sprinkled more cinnamon, then began to braid.

Home is what we could have together, but you're too afraid to build it.

She ignored the longing that twisted in her chest and thought about how she could get Maxim out of the house. Would it be too cold for him to sleep in the dairy barn? Probably. She didn't have any fuel for the heaters out there. Conserving heat in a limited space was the only way she managed to survive on her own during the weeks around Midwinter. She had fuel and food, but only for herself. She would need to go hunting.

Or you could kick him out.

Impossible. Her traitor heart rebelled at the thought. Her traitor heart was the one who'd led her down the stairs the night before, longing for the comfort of Max's arms. Her traitor heart would give the man everything if she let it.

She finished the loaf and put it in a long proofing basket. It would be ready to bake that night. Ready to eat in the days leading up to Midwinter.

Midwinter.

The night she'd finally lost everything.

Renata closed her eyes and clutched the edge of the counter. Why had he come? Hadn't she hurt him enough? It was only going to get worse. She was weak and he knew it. If he pushed hard enough, she'd give him everything. Again.

And then what?

Force him to live a half-life with a broken mate? Unacceptable. Force her back into a world where all the rules she'd known were upended?

Renata was still coming to terms with the new order in the Irin world. Grigori—once their hated foes—had now proven that not all of them were murderous monsters. The Grigori Max had met so many years ago in Prague hadn't been lying. Some Grigori even had sisters to protect, half-angelic daughters tormented by humanity's soul voices because they had no control over their magic.

It wasn't that she was unsympathetic. She had plenty of sympathy. For the women.

For the Grigori? How was she supposed to quash her instinctive, murderous impulses when she smelled the scent of sandalwood? Would their unnatural beauty ever cause her anything but cold rage? The scraping sound of their soul voices made her nauseous.

It might have been the mandate of the council that free Grigori who were living peaceful lives could be Irin allies, but no one had asked the Irina who survived their murderous rampage, had they?

Was she supposed to forget two hundred years of training and go back to singing songs?

She wasn't the woman she'd been. She never would be again. That girl had died with Balien. Maybe now that Max had found this haven and taken away her last hiding place, she would have to move on. Maybe it was better that she lose this sanctuary.

You keep looking for the same feeling you lost, but you won't find it because it was never the building.

He was right. Max was right. She simply didn't know where else to go.

Renata wiped her eyes and walked to the cold storage. There was cured sausage and cheese to eat, along with a loaf of bread she'd cooked yesterday. She'd eat a little bit and set out the rest for Max when he returned from exploring the caves. He was a curious man—it was one of the things she loved about him—and Renata suspected he could spend days just reading the spells along the walls. She didn't need to read them. She'd spent two hundred years reading them and hoping they'd give her peace. They hadn't. She doubted she'd ever find peace again.

———————

MAX RETURNED from the caves while she was reading a book by the fire.

"There is food set out in the kitchen," she said quietly, not looking up.

"Thank you." He didn't go to the kitchen. He crossed the living room and sprawled on the couch, forcing his head into her lap. "That library must have been remarkable."

She put her book down, knowing he took pleasure in distracting her. "It was."

"Has no one come back in over two hundred years? No one even came looking for the scrolls?"

"Maybe." She combed her fingers through Max's thick blond hair. It was wavy—almost curly—and shone gold in the firelight. "I didn't return to this place for over one hundred years. Someone might have been back before that, but they would have seen everything gone."

"Not everything." He grabbed her hand. Kissed her palm. "I can still feel so much joy in that place. The magic in the walls is still vibrant."

Renata closed her hand, curling her fingers into her palm. "I only feel pain. Loss."

"There are both. Pain and joy. That is life. There's something in the tunnels I want you to—"

"Don't make me go back there." She sighed. "Max, I know I can't get rid of you, but can you just..."

"What?"

"Let me be." She closed her eyes. "Just let me be. Ignore me. You are welcome to stay here and rest. Explore the library as much as you want. Eat my food. But let me be. If you need to, pretend I'm not here."

He nipped the heel of her hand with his teeth. "Well, that would be idiotic."

She frowned. "Why?"

"Because I didn't come here for a quiet mountain getaway, Reni. I didn't come to explore a library. I came for you."

"You came to prove you could find me. To prove that you're a better tracker than I am."

Max flipped, grabbed Renata by the waist, and pulled her under his body. The move was so fluid she blinked, and he was leaning over her, his shoulders so broad he blocked the light.

"You think you know why I came here?"

She couldn't not react. He was too vital. Too desirable. Too much of everything she admired.

"We aren't this," she said. "We never were."

He cocked his head. "Where have you been the past eighteen years?"

Running away from you.

"I've been living my life, Max. A life that you've only ever touched the edges of."

"I know I don't know everything about you. That's what makes it fun. I don't mind secrets, because I like finding answers."

"Oh? And what happens when you find everything? You move on to the next challenge?"

"I might if I didn't think the woman I was chasing didn't have a thousand new ways to surprise me." Max leaned down, his lips inches from hers. "Is this your argument, Reni? Is this the best you've got? Do you really think I'm going to get bored? That's insulting to both of us. Is that the excuse you've been using all this time? That I have a short attention span?"

No. When Max was on a hunt, his failing was extreme focus, not short attention span.

Renata said, "I think you don't know what it means to be in a relationship. It's not all chases and excitement."

"We have a relationship. Don't fool yourself. And we did just fine in Vienna. It wasn't all chases and excitement there. It was long days and frustrations and bitching about our bosses, as the humans say. Guess what? Still wasn't bored, Renata. I still wanted more."

Damn her heart. "You're right. You should have more." She gently shoved him to the side and stood. "I need to put the bread in the oven."

SHE LET him stay in her room that night. It would have been pointless to have him sleep downstairs when she'd end up beside him eventually. Max didn't gloat. He simply moved his backpack up to her room and made himself at home, as if it was his right.

It was far too easy to fall into the familiar patterns they'd begun to establish in Vienna. She knew what side of the bed he liked and how affectionate he was in the morning. He dropped off to sleep quickly at the end of the day but would laze in bed every morning, given the chance. She knew he was fastidious about brushing his teeth and would wake at the slightest sound in the night, slide on his boots, and be halfway to the door before she opened her eyes.

He was sleeping with his arm around her waist, one leg thrown over hers as if trying to keep her in place. Renata was not sleeping at all. There'd been something in the caves earlier that had caught her attention, but she'd been too distracted by having Max there to pay attention.

"Bread." She glanced at Max, but he didn't wake.

The smell of fresh bread had been in the tunnels. She was sure of it. She'd dismissed it initially because she assumed what she'd caught a hint of was herself. She'd been baking so much that week it was an easy mistake to make. But the smell in the tunnels was too fresh. She hadn't baked that morning, not until she'd left the caves.

Gently, she lifted Max's arm and slid out from under his hold. He shifted, pressed his face into her pillow, then let out a long sigh. Renata walked to the door and opened it, grateful that the caretaker regularly oiled the hinges. She walked downstairs, wrapping a woolen shawl around her, and put on her boots before she made her way down the hall. She grabbed a flashlight this time. She didn't want to use magic when she was trying to examine a scene.

Renata slowly walked through the reading room and down the hall, opening her senses to her surroundings.

Nothing. The library was as cold and lifeless as a grave.

Has no one come back?

She didn't want this place filled with voices again. Didn't want new songs to fill the hall. It would have seemed as irreverent as a feast on a grave.

Renata walked back to the children's tunnels and paused at the entrance, sure she didn't want to follow through but certain this

65

was the place where she'd caught the scent earlier in the day. It was gone now, but she could swear she heard the stomp of running feet and the sound of childish laughter.

Relentless curiosity won out over the ghosts.

She walked back, carefully examining each room with the clinical eye of an investigator. By the time she reached the end, she was certain someone had been in the caves. There was little dust and the air wasn't stale.

She turned to the last door on the left and hesitated. Images of empty clothes and abandoned shoes filled her mind. Gold dust in the air and blood spattering the walls.

With a scream trapped in her heart, she walked in. She kept her eyes from the corner opposite the door and swept her flashlight along the far wall. It was empty. No clothes. No shoes. No blood. Mala had been the one to clear this room. Renata hadn't had the courage.

Her flashlight stopped on the table. Paper and colored pencils. Mala was an artist, but these didn't look like her work. These drawings could only have been made by a child.

Renata walked closer and slid them across the table. Most were animals. A cow with a bright bell around its neck. A lion. A well-rendered stag and a flock of sheep on a mountainside. The last one was a bright red fox with his head lifted in a howl, the artist dropping the brown colored pencil in the middle of a stroke, as if she had been interrupted.

What was this?

There had been nothing left like this after the Rending. The colored pencils were new. Modern. She'd seen that brand in the shops in the village.

She lifted her flashlight and turned it around the room. When her flashlight illuminated the mural, she froze.

Mala had cleaned the room, but she'd done something more. The painting filled a wall that had been covered in blood and little handprints. The wall was warped by Renata's scream when she'd discovered it. The surface had buckled with her magic, like a body absorbing the force of a blow. What once had been smooth had become rippled and jagged.

But Mala had transformed that wall. She'd smoothed the cracks into gentle ripples and covered the blood with bright paint. She'd turned the room of horrors into a place of peace by capturing the beauty of the mountains around them. She'd filled it with creation instead of death. The children and animals sprang to life in the dark cave, so vibrant they'd inspired a small artist to copy small pieces of them with childish hands.

Renata's emotions ricocheted between anger and wonder.

Who had invaded this place?

The mural was so beautiful. So peaceful.

Was it a child? How had a child gotten into the caves?

She needed to thank Mala, but thanks wasn't enough.

Did one of the renters—

"We really do make the best team," Max said quietly from the door.

Renata lifted her eyes to him and he blocked the glare of her flashlight. He was wearing a pair of linen pants and nothing else. She dropped the beam to his feet and ignored the instant surge of lust his exposed body provoked. Her emotions were running high.

"Did you see this earlier?" she asked.

"Yes. It's what I wanted to show you."

"You should have insisted."

"I would have, but you were in full avoidance mode. I thought it would be better to wait."

She left it alone because he was right and she didn't want to admit it.

"Bread," Renata said. "It smelled like bread in the corridor."

"I noticed it too." Max stepped into the room and set a lamp on the table. The low light illuminated the room, bringing harsh shadows to soft light. "Did Mala paint this?"

"She must have."

"It's beautiful."

Renata didn't look at the mural again. If she looked at it, her heart would break open and she didn't—couldn't—do that again. Her grief would bury her. Bury them. "Do you think one of the renters might have broken in?"

"Possibly." Max looked around. "These tunnels are too well ventilated not to have some network of side passages."

"They do. There's an extensive network of caverns, but I thought we'd blocked the entrances."

"Perhaps a child could still fit through."

"And the scent of bread?"

Max shrugged. "Renata, you know as much as I do. It's the middle of the night and it's snowing again. If anyone is in these caverns tonight, they must desperately need shelter. Why don't we go to bed and we'll look more in the morning?"

"I won't be able to sleep."

Max held out his hand. "Come with me."

She didn't want to leave, but she knew staying in the mural room would only break her open. And that did not need to happen. Especially not with Max around. She took his hand, and Max picked up the lamp, guiding them out of the corridor and through the library. He secured the iron lock when they made it back to the house, then handed her the lamp.

"Hold this."

"Why?"

He didn't answer, just walked into the music room without her. He returned carrying an old guitar.

"Do you play?" Renata was shocked. She hadn't known that about him.

"A little. I only know a few songs. You can't sleep? I'll see if my bad playing can make you drift off from boredom."

She doubted that. Renata loved music, but she didn't like to admit it. The thought of Maxim playing...

"You're thoughtful," she said. "That should bore me in no time."

"I aim to please."

HE PLAYED, but it wasn't boring or amateurish. It was beautiful.

"You've played a long time."

"No. Yes." He shook his head. "I played a long time ago. My grandfather taught me. It was the only thing he taught me other than how to throw an ax."

"He raised you."

"He fed us. Protected us. But... he was quite shattered by his daughters' deaths. My mother and Leo's were twin sisters and his only children. He thought we'd all died for a long time."

She frowned. "What do you mean?"

"We were only babies during the Rending. Both of us were born the same summer. When our village was attacked, everyone died. Or so the scribe house in Riga thought. We were gone for two years after the Rending, and then... we weren't. Someone left us at the scribe house, and my grandfather was notified. Leo's father returned from Russia a few years later—we'd all thought he died too—but he never really spoke again. He taught us to fight. He was... frightening. As frightening as Leo is gentle. But my grandfather stayed with us. Sometimes I think he was afraid of what my uncle would do if he wasn't there."

"There were no Irina?"

Max shook his head and began plucking the strings in a delicate tune.

"What is that?" she asked.

"A Russian folk song."

"It's beautiful."

The ghost of a smile on his face. "I'm glad you like it."

"Your mother and your aunt? You don't remember anything? Where were you for two years? Who took care of you?"

"I remember someone playing guitar." He smiled. "But after the Rending? I remember a little. Or I think I do. I'm not certain."

"What do you remember?"

"Fear." He stopped playing. "Screaming. Then silence. A lot of silence. Leo and I were in a dark place. I think someone must have hidden us somewhere. I remember the cold. It was cold at night, even in the summer. I dream about a boy with silver hair and gold eyes. I don't know if they're memories or dreams. Or visions. Wolves in the snow and a boy with gold eyes sitting by a fire, feeding us milk."

"Gold eyes could mean—"

"*Kareshta?*" He started playing again. "I thought of that after I learned of their existence. *Kareshta* would have been able to care for us without hurting themselves like humans would, but I'm quite certain it's a boy in my dreams. So I don't know what to think."

Renata's mind whirled with the possibilities.

"I don't have many distinct memories of my childhood after that. We were raised in the scribe house because there was no other place to keep us. So we were always around warriors with my grandfather and my uncle. Neither of them are talkative men. I know next to nothing about my mother or my aunt."

Max started playing again, and Renata watched him silently. The song was a low, aching ballad. His fingers plucked the strings delicately, matching the mournful, crying wind of the storm. He'd never put a shirt back on, so her eyes feasted on him as he played. He was a banquet of rippling muscle and smooth skin turned gold in the lamplight. His eyes were closed as he played, and his top teeth gripped his bottom lip in concentration.

He was so beautiful it made her heart ache.

What would it be like to remember so little? To carry an empty pack through your life? Would it be a light journey or a lonely one?

Max paused. "I think what I'm most afraid of in this life is that I will get to the end of it—die in battle or just from exhaustion—and have no memories of home."

Renata's voice was hardly a whisper. "I have memories, but they bring me no joy."

His voice hardened. "Is that why I'm so angry with you, Reni? You know what home is, and you reject it. You played for years—showing me peeks of a life with you—then you passed judgment. You told me what we had wasn't good enough. 'Move on, Maxim. You'll never compare to what I lost.'"

CHAPTER SIX

Max propped the guitar in the corner and walked to Renata. She didn't want to sleep? Fine.

He pulled her to her knees on the bed and grasped her hip in one hand and her neck in the other. His kiss landed on her lips with the force of the wind battering the house. She met his passion with her own, wrapping her arms around his waist and sliding her hands down into the back of his pants, gripping his buttocks and bringing his hips to meet hers.

Max shoved Renata back on the bed and fell on top of her, searching for skin. She was still covered in a flannel nightdress and he hated it. Hated everything that kept her body from meeting his skin. Hated the distance between them. Her stubbornness. His resentment. Max sat back and grasped the bottom of the night-dress, shoving it up Renata's body.

"Get rid of it."

She pulled the flannel over her head and then she was his, lying before him, a dream of dark hair and long legs. Her reddish-brown hair splayed across the pillow. Her eyes were heavy and her lips already swollen from his kiss.

"I'm going to look at you," he said. "It's been two years, ten months, and four days since I've had the pleasure of it."

"You're—"

"Hard as iron?" He grasped his erection. "That's not going anywhere." He ran his palms from her knees up to her hips. "You, on the other hand, have a tendency to disappear."

Max lifted her ankle to his shoulder and scraped his teeth on the tender skin behind her knee. She always jumped when he did that, and this night was no different. She reached for him, but he batted her hand away and pressed down on her belly, keeping her immobile as she lay before him. He played his tongue along her leg, up her thigh, tasting the arousal hidden by the soft hair between her thighs, but only long enough to leave her twisting. Then he spread her legs and kissed his way up her body.

"Max—"

"Quiet," he said in a low voice as he shoved her knees open and settled between her thighs. "Did you miss me, Renata?" He guided himself into her body as her hips arched up and she let out a low gasp. "Did you miss this?" He seated himself to the hilt inside her, thrusting into her as he held her knee up, opening her body to him. "Did you?"

"Yes," she hissed. Renata closed her eyes, her face a mask of tension and pleasure.

"Open your eyes."

She obeyed him. Renata's eyes met his, her gaze swimming in hunger, heat, and anger. She dug her nails into his buttocks, pulling him harder into her body with each thrust.

"*Lisitsa*," he said with a grim smile. "Don't you know I like your teeth?"

"Shut up."

"No." He took her mouth again, biting her lower lip as he rode her. He ground into her body, searching for the telltale signs she was near her climax. The hitched breath. The cry. The tightening of her body around him and the way her fingers dug into the small of his back.

He had been her lover for eighteen years. He knew every sign. Every tell.

"Don't look away from me," he said when she closed her eyes. "Don't try to hide."

She was the first and only woman he had ever dreamed about, the only one he obsessed over. Again and again, he returned to her, even when she pushed him away. Since the return of the Irina, there were others who had approached him, but none had been her equal.

He felt her climax approaching and he slowed his thrusts, smiling when she beat his shoulders.

"Don't you dare!" she commanded him. "Faster."

Max bent down and bit her shoulder as he picked up the pace, twisting his hips when he heard her cry out. She was so close.

"Maxim." She panted his name. "Please."

He could feel his *talesm* rising. Feel the magic thick in the air around them. If she were his mate, her marks would be glowing too. Their power would intertwine in this moment, and he would see his vow written over her heart, see his marks glow on her body. But the only mark she bore was that of her intended mate—a simple, spare circle on her forehead.

Max braced himself over Renata and let instinct take control of his body. He closed his eyes and lost himself in the pleasure. There was no thought. No calculation. He felt his release gathering. It was a wave, rising and cresting.

Her back arched when she came, and she cried out his name. He opened his eyes to watch her. Tears leaked from the corners of her eyes. Relief? Pleasure?

Max didn't know, but he gave in to it, capturing her mouth as his climax crested and crashed. Renata captured his guttural cry and swallowed it, her hand grasping the back of his neck to keep their mouths fused together.

Needing air, he pulled away. Max pressed his forehead against hers, to the mark another man had drawn. A mark that still glowed when he made love to her.

"Maxim," she whispered, panting. "Max, I—"

"How long did he love you?" Max closed his eyes. "Two years? The blink of an eye. I've loved you so much longer."

She froze beneath him, their bodies still linked.

"How many times did you cry out his name when he brought you pleasure? Not as many times as you've shouted mine."

"Stop it." Her voice was cold.

Max opened his eyes and saw the tears coursing down her cheeks, but his heart was raw. "Am I good enough yet? Have I loved you enough? Or am I only good for this?" He bucked his hips against hers. "Because nothing will ever compare to a *reshon* you loved and lost."

He knew he'd hurt her, but the look in her eyes was only a shadow of the pain he'd felt when she rejected him in Vienna. When she'd told him his love wasn't real, it had gutted him.

Max couldn't take any more. He lifted off her body and wrapped a sheet around his waist as Renata scrambled to cover herself. The pleasure was hollow. He'd lost his temper and been too honest. Too rough. She'd probably never let him touch her again.

Maybe that was all right.

"I'm going outside for a smoke," he said. "Don't worry; I'll sleep on the couch."

MAX SAT on the covered porch that wrapped around the house. Heavy boards were nailed along the railings, creating a buffer from the wind and harsh snow. The storm that had picked up earlier in the evening had cleared, though Max could see more dark clouds over the far ridge. For the moment, the air was crisp and clear and the moon was full, glittering over the fresh snow in the meadow.

He sat on a log bench and blew out a stream of smoke from the cigarettes he'd bought in Milan. They were a fancy variety and an indulgence. He didn't smoke often, but the scent reminded him of his grandfather's pipe tobacco, and it was welcome on the cold night.

If the weather was clear, he'd hike down the mountain in the morning.

He was a fool.

Renata had dug into her anger and grief like the ancient singers had dug into the mountain. It was part of her, and he was only an amusement. He'd never be enough for her, because she'd tasted life with her *reshon*. Making love to him probably felt like a shadow of the connection they'd had, even if it was life changing for Max.

Yes, he was a fool. A fool for loving Renata for so long when she didn't want to be loved. A fool for pursuing her across continents and up the side of a mountain. He should have believed her eighteen years ago and cut his losses. Maybe if he'd done that, he'd have found a mate who wanted him instead of a lover who tolerated him.

Maybe some griefs you simply didn't recover from. Perhaps some lives were lost, even if the bodies stayed breathing. Renata had always felt so alive to him. Passionate and angry and joyous and fierce. But maybe he was only seeing what he needed to see and not what was actually there.

Max heard Renata's footsteps on the stairs and knew from the speed and the hard stomp that she was angry. Furious.

He rose and turned toward the door a second before she flung it open.

"Fuck you!" she yelled, stepping onto the porch. "I've never once thought of Balien when we were making love. So fuck you, Maxim!"

His eyes went wide. "Get inside," he yelled.

"No!"

"You're going to freeze to death." He flicked his cigarette into the snow and picked her up. "Are you insane?"

"Put me down," she yelled. "I was born in these mountains, and I'm not going to freeze. I'm not some delicate lowland—"

"It is below freezing out here and there is more snow coming." He rushed her into the house and kicked the kitchen door closed. Then he took her to the fire and grabbed a woolen throw from the back of the couch. "You're insane."

"And you're an ass."

"So you've told me many times."

"You think you can throw all that on me and I'm just supposed to take it?"

He grabbed another blanket. "Shut up and get closer to the fire."

"I'm fine."

"You're not fine. You're naked."

"I have a sheet on. Just like you did when you walked out on me upstairs. Just like you walked out on me in Vienna."

He sat back on his heels, mouth gaping. "Walked out on *you*?"

She muttered, "You were sitting out there brooding and thinking about ways to get down the mountain just now, weren't you?"

"You told me in Vienna that I didn't know what love was and I'd never compare to your lost *reshon*. Was I supposed to stick around after that?"

"You were supposed to find someone else!" Her eyes flashed. "You were supposed to find someone better, Max. I don't want to rob you of the chance to—"

"What? Find my *reshon*? This shit again?"

"It's not shit, and the fact that you think it is—"

"I don't *want* some mythical woman who might not even exist!" He rose and gripped his hair. "Don't you understand that? What about us is so horrible?"

"That's not—"

"We laugh together. We fight together. I adore your cooking and think the fact that you have the patience of a gnat is hilarious, even when it drives me crazy. I love that you like a snowstorm more than a beach and you consider dagger fighting a sport. I love that you are fiercely compassionate and protective of your sisters. I love *you*! I love everything about you, even the parts that make me insane."

"You say that because you don't know. You deserve—"

"I deserve *you*." He caged her on the sofa with his arms. "Because you're the one I want. I don't need anyone else. And I know you love me too." He leaned in. "I know you do. That's what makes me so damn crazy."

She shoved him back and tore off the blankets he'd wrapped around her. "Of course I love you! That's why I know this isn't good enough, Max. I know I make you crazy. I know we drive each other up the wall. You want to live with that the rest of your life?"

He was struck dumb. *Of course I love you.* It was the first time she'd actually said it.

"There is a woman out there," she continued, "created by heaven, who will be your perfect mate." She choked on the last word and Max's heart broke. "She's made for you, Maxim. She will love you in ways I never could."

Max whispered, "Renata."

"Don't!" She held up a hand. "I want you to imagine that for a moment. Really and truly imagine it. Imagine marking me as your mate. You can't take that back, Max. That bond is only broken in death. Imagine marking me and then meeting *her*."

Max wanted to put his mark on her more than anything in their dark and twisted world, but Renata was still talking.

"If I let this happen," she continued, "let *us* happen—you will meet her and resent me for eternity for stealing that from you. Always knowing that she was your best match, your truest match, but instead you mated me." She blinked away tears. "Are *you* enough? Max, that was never the question."

"Don't do this to us." He walked to her and put his hands on her shoulders. "If you love me, don't push me away."

She pressed her hand over his heart. "I need to do what is right, even if you don't understand why."

Heaven above, her fierce heart. Renata had walls—plenty of them—but she was so ferociously protective. She owned him.

"You're thinking about this backward," Max said.

"What are you talking about?"

"Has it never occurred to you that my *reshon* was lost too?"

Her eyes went wide, and Max knew it had never crossed her mind.

"Renata, most of the women in our race were killed during the Rending. The Irin birth rate dropped almost to nothing after the Irina went into hiding. Maybe I do have a *reshon* out there, but the chances are greater that she's gone."

She said nothing, but he could see that his words had made an impact.

"Thousands of Irin have met and mated through our history with the mate of their choice. No one is guaranteed a *reshon*."

Her face remained carefully blank.

"But beyond all that," Max said, "we are creatures of free will. That is the gift that separates us from the monsters. And if we have a will, then my choice is you. It will always be you." Max bent and kissed Renata's forehead right over Balien's mark. "And I'm sorry. I am sorry, Renata. I was angry and I shouldn't have used him against you. That was wrong."

"I've never compared you to Balien," she said woodenly. "That's not what this is about."

"What we have—right here, right now, with each other—is precious. Maybe we aren't *reshon*, but you can't tell me we're not meant. I love you and I want a life with you. I don't want to wait when heaven has already given me a precious gift."

She shook her head. "But if she is out there—"

"If she's out there, then nothing. It's you I want." He squeezed her shoulders. "I would have you as my mate, Renata. I want that more than anything. And nothing would change that bond. You are my choice. You are the one I want. That is all that matters."

Renata was silent.

"Say it again," he whispered.

She frowned.

"Tell me you love me," he said. "I've been waiting to hear it for a very long time."

"I love you." Her eyes were defiant and still a little angry. "Don't ever question that."

"And I love you. Think about *that* when you decide if you're willing to make a home with me. Don't think about what might be. Think about what is." He wrapped his arms around her. "And you're right. I *was* thinking about hiking down the mountain, but you changed my mind. You're stuck with me now."

THEY MADE love in front of the fire, and this time Max fell asleep with Renata wrapped in his arms. They slept long and hard, through the early morning when the snow and wind returned. They lay tangled together in front of the fire and listened to the wind together.

Sometime around dawn the next morning, Renata sang a soft song about Midwinter Night and the stars shining from the heavens. It was a song of praise and thanksgiving and hope for longer and brighter days ahead.

Outside of battle songs, it was the first time Max had heard her sing.

CHAPTER SEVEN

"Why are we doing this?" She tromped up the hill behind the house.

"Because it's a lovely tradition, it's cheerful, and if we don't get some fresh air in the next few hours, we're going to be out of luck for the next day."

Renata could see the storm clouds moving across a distant ridge. Max was right. They'd slept through the early morning and woken together when the sun was high. And though it was shining off the newly fallen snow at the moment, by evening another wave of the storm would be on them.

"Christmas trees are a human tradition."

"So?" Max grinned. "Irin already cut branches to bring in the house for Midwinter. This is just... a little more greenery."

"It's a tree. In the house." Even though she didn't quite understand why Max wanted to participate in the human tradition of a Christmas tree, she nevertheless scanned the slopes for a suitable specimen. "Is this Ava's doing?"

Ava was mated to Malachi, one of Maxim's brothers. They lived together in Istanbul at the scribe house, but Ava had grown up in the human world and still identified strongly with it, even after discovering her magic.

"Ava started it a few years ago in Prague, right before the babies were born, but we kept it up. The children like it, and it's cheerful." Max put his hands on his hips and squinted at the snow-covered slopes. "We often have to drive quite far for a tree at home, but there are so many here."

"Yes, the humans here have their pick of trees to kill." She walked over to one that looked appropriate. "This one?" It was a few inches taller than she was and would reach nearly to the rafters.

Max said, "Are you sure you want one that big?"

"If we're going to cut one, we shouldn't cut a small one." She cocked her head. "And this will smell lovely in the house. I do love the smell."

He walked around the tree, and Renata watched him as he examined it. He'd wrapped up in his parka and boots, leaving his head bare because they weren't walking far. His dark blond hair shone in the sun, and his skin, naturally pale, was ruddy and sun-kissed.

Max had always been one of the most attractive men she'd ever known. All Irin were naturally handsome because of their angelic blood, but even among them, Max stood out.

He caught her watching him. "What?" He brushed his hair. "I was crawling in the brush."

Renata shook her head. "You don't have anything in your hair."

He frowned. "Then—"

"You would make beautiful children," she said quickly. "That's all I was thinking."

"I would with you." Color rode high on his cheekbones. "Do you want children?"

She hadn't allowed herself to think about it. The only man she wanted was Max, and Max had never been hers. Renata had been convinced that one day she would hear about him meeting his *reshon* and mating. Probably Sari would tell her. Or Ava. Someone would casually let it drop in conversation. Renata had forced herself to imagine it over and over, forming different scenarios as if preparation would guard her heart from devastation.

Because losing him *would* devastate her. She'd been prepared for that. What she hadn't been prepared for was a future with him.

"I don't know if I want children," she said. "What I do—what *we* do isn't friendly to family life. My roots were torn once. I don't know if I want new ones."

Max paused. "You know... it used to be that scribes and singers would take sabbaticals to bear children. They would find a place— sometimes isolated like this—and have their children quietly. Raise them until they were independent and ready for training. For boys, it's only thirteen years before we enter training."

"For girls it depends on geography. I never left home."

"Because you were preparing to follow your mother as an archivist."

She nodded. "I know what you're saying. We live long lives. Raising children is a short season."

"We could come here, Renata. Or we could raise our children in Istanbul with Ava and Malachi's. Join the community there."

She felt her heart pick up when he said "our children."

"Or we could choose to simply be." Max walked around the tree toward her. "Children are never guaranteed for our kind. Don't ever think that you aren't enough, Reni. You have always been enough for me."

She leaned her forehead into his chest. *How can I be enough?*

"I love you," he whispered. "You will always be enough."

What if Max was right? What if they had both lost their chance of a soul mate? Renata knew that she'd never love another scribe the way she loved Max. Her fear had been that he would find better. Find *his* best.

But what if it really was her?

"Are you frightened?" he asked.

"Yes. Aren't you?"

"I'm only frightened you'll leave again," he said. "I've chased you for a long time."

She lifted her head and met his eyes. "This was my last hiding place."

His eyes danced. "As if you couldn't find another."

"I'm tired of running from you." She leaned forward and took his mouth in a long kiss. His lips were warm and dry. Heat radiated from his chest and arms as he put them around her. Renata's head spun. From pleasure or lack of air, she couldn't quite tell. When they broke apart, Max was smiling as she gasped for air.

"You wanted to be caught."

"Maybe. I suppose if I hadn't, I would have shot you the first time you found me." She closed her eyes and leaned on his shoulder "What do you want from me, Maxim?"

"I want you to give us a chance," he said. "I want to love you when you don't have one foot out the door like you did in Vienna. I want you to move to Istanbul and live with me and help me in my work. Help Leo and Kyra train *kareshta*. Help me gather information about Grigori who are threats. You don't have to stay in one place—you're not that kind of woman—but I want to know that when you're ready to come home, you're coming to me."

As he listed his wishes, Renata realized that what Max really wanted was a commitment. He wanted Renata to risk that his love would last. That it wouldn't be usurped by an interloper who might or might not exist. He wanted her to trust him.

When she thought about it that way, the answer was obvious. Max was the most stubbornly faithful man she'd ever met. She'd trust him with her life. More, she'd trust her sisters' lives to him.

"Yes," she said simply. "We should cut this one and get back to the house." She stepped back and looked at the tree, holding her hand out for the ax Max was carrying. "May I?"

His mouth was hanging open. "What?"

"We should cut this one. Unless there is something wrong with the other side. You looked at it. I did not."

"You said yes."

"I did." And part of her soul was crouched in fear. She felt as if she'd stripped to her skin and walked into the storm that was coming for them.

"You'll move to Istanbul?"

She nodded. "It's a reasonable suggestion and a good base. I have no problem working with Malachi."

"You'll help Leo and Kyra."

"When I can."

He dropped the ax and reached for her hand. "You'll come home with me."

"And I'll leave again." She looked at him. "Understand that, Maxim. I won't be with you every moment. I was that girl once; I'm not anymore. I need to be useful, which means that sometimes I'll leave. Sometimes you'll come with me. Or I'll go with you. But sometimes I won't be able to tell you where I'm going and I'll have to go alone."

His hand gripped her fingers. "But you'll come home."

"I will come home. So if you want to be that home, then I say yes. I'll come home to you."

THEY SPENT the afternoon cleaning and decorating the tree, cutting paper garlands from stacks of newspaper piled by the fire, making stars out of sticks and thread, and finding small candles to light the branches. They set the tree in the corner, and Max decorated it while Renata cut bread and opened cans of oily sardines and oysters one of the renters had left. She set out a tray with oysters, olives, apples, and roasted hazelnuts.

"We should be fine as long as you like bread," she said. "There's plenty of flour and oil. The meat I brought will last for another week or so. The previous renters left quite a few cans of these. The apples won't last long though."

"Is there hunting here?"

Renata nodded. "There's good hunting if the weather clears. Deer and chamois, mostly. I can set out traps for rabbits." She could feel his eyes on her. "What?"

"You're very easy to live with," he said. "I remember from Vienna. Not everyone is."

"I thought the same about you."

"Did you live with Balien?"

Her chest tightened, but she forced herself to take deep breaths.

Max said, "It still bothers you to talk about him."

"It bothers me to talk about the past," she said. "It's not him in particular. And no. My parents were traditional. We wouldn't live together until we were mated, though we shared rooms when we traveled. That wasn't an issue."

"Why didn't you mate?"

Renata laughed a little. "Not everyone is so eager to jump into mating. I wanted to meet Balien's family. And later, he was worried that mating with me..."

"You both would have been weaker for a time."

She nodded. "It didn't seem like a good idea when we were running."

Max turned back to the tree, hanging red paper stars on the top branches. "I'm giving us six months."

Renata blinked. "What?"

"Six months," he said. "After that, the world might be falling apart, but I'm taking you away and making you mine. My brothers will have to understand."

"Six months is not very long."

He frowned. "How about six months and eighteen years? Is that long enough to know if someone is your mate?"

Her cheeks reddened. "I suppose you have a point. Still, we

don't know what will be happening in six months. It might not be a good time—"

"No." Max walked over and pulled her up by her hand. "Six months, Renata. I knew years ago we were suited. I'm not willing to wait longer to appease someone else's schedule or plans. You are my priority. When it comes to you, I will be entirely selfish."

"You're important to your watcher."

"And you're important to me." He kissed her and let her go. "Six months."

She snuggled into his side, looking at the tiny lights on the tree as they sat by the fire.

"Admit it."

Renata didn't feel like arguing. "You're right. It's lovely and a wonderful tradition. Though I'll be sweeping up pine needles for weeks."

"Worth it. I'll vacuum them up too. The tree is perfect."

She cocked her head. "It does look very nice there."

"Our dinner was delicious. And the bread you have baking smells heavenly." He nuzzled her hair. "Almost as heavenly as you."

"The bread is far, far sweeter," she said with a laugh.

He leaned back and looked at her. "What is that expression? I don't think I recognize it."

"I'm... happy."

"Are you?" He played with her hair.

"Don't tease."

"I wouldn't dare." He settled back beside her. "I could become accustomed to Happy Renata."

Midwinter was the next day, but though the wind had picked up, she was feeling light. She was letting herself imagine a future with Max, and she liked her imagination. For the first time in two hundred years, she wasn't faced with an endless dark night on Midwinter. She felt hope.

"Is it your mother's honey bread recipe that you're baking?"

She nodded.

"She'd be pleased you remember it after so many years."

"I baked it with her every year. How could I forget?"

The memory that had marked Renata as an archivist from the time she was a child became a curse after the Rending. She could remember every moment and every horror just as she remembered every joy and every verse of Irina songs and histories. If she was stronger, she would have composed a lament and let their history be sung and shared with those who also endured grief.

She hadn't done that. She'd locked the memories away.

"What are you thinking?" Max said.

"My mother would not be proud of me," she whispered.

"How can you say that?"

She closed her eyes. "It was my duty to remember and sing the songs. That is what she did. What her grandmother did. Her great-aunt. All the women of our family who are gone now. I was the only one left, and it was my duty to write the songs of the Rending for those who were there and those who weren't. I was an archivist. To have healing, our people need a lament."

"Others have written laments."

"But not mine," she whispered. "Not mine."

"You couldn't forget what happened here if you tried." Max kissed her temple. "When you're ready, you'll write your lament, and I will listen to every note. I'll hold you while you sing it if you need me to. Others will listen and hear and remember. But to sing it properly, you have to sing the joy as well as the sorrow. I think you've remembered the sorrow but not the joy that preceded it. Centuries of joy and learning and life, Renata. I felt it in the library. Don't forget to sing that too."

She glanced at the table under the window where the seven-branched candelabra should sit. She'd hidden it back in the caves once Max had come, unwilling to face any reminders of the Midwinter holiday when her defenses were so low.

Renata stood and wrapped a woolen throw around herself.

"What are you doing?"

"I put the joy away," she said. "Can you come help me get it out of storage?"

Max stood with a smile. "Absolutely."

They walked back to the library, leaving the heavy iron door open. A gust of cool air brushed Renata's face as she entered the reading room, and she was reminded of the pictures in the classroom.

"We'll need to close off the back tunnels," she said. "I'm sure whoever was here doesn't mean any harm, but it's really not safe to be exploring back in the caverns unless you know where you're going."

"After the storm," Max said. "Whoever is breaking in hasn't harmed anything, and the last thing they need to deal with is finding another shelter in weather like this."

She walked to the cabinets where she'd stored the silver as Max walked toward the back hallway. She didn't love the idea of anyone trespassing on her family history, but she knew Max was right. Nothing good could come of taking away shelter in a storm. What disturbed her more was the artist who'd drawn the pictures.

"Whoever has been visiting brought a child with them," she said. "These caverns are not safe for a child."

Max was standing in the hallway, staring at something on the ground. "There's a child."

"I know. I just said—"

"Renata," he hissed. Max was pointing at the ground. "There is a *child*."

Her eyes dropped to the ground. In the alcove, surrounded by a cozy nest of blankets, lay a child of no more than eight or nine, sleeping soundly. It appeared to be a female with tangled hair falling over her face.

Renata walked toward Max, stopping when she saw the girl's breath hitch. She and Max froze. The girl stopped breathing.

Then her eyes flew open, she sat bolt upright, and a scream of terror echoed through the library. Renata fell back against a wall and felt it warp under her hands as the girl's fear manifested. A punch of magic hit Renata in the solar plexus, leaving her breathless. Even Max stumbled back.

In the space of a heartbeat, the child bolted up and disappeared into the darkness of the caves. Max started to run after her, but Renata held him back.

"No!" she shouted. "She's terrified of you. Of us."

"What was that?"

"She's *kareshta*." Renata ran her hands along the hallway walls, her eyes wide and wondering.

"What? How do you—?"

"Look at the stone, Max. That child has magic, and it's very, very powerful."

CHAPTER EIGHT

Max and Renata walked back to the house.

"There's climbing equipment in the storeroom, Renata said. "We'll need it if we're going back to the caverns."

"Are you sure about this?"

"You felt her magic, Max."

"I know. I just... If she doesn't want to be found—"

"She *needs* to be found. It's not safe."

Renata opened the door opposite the music room, and Max saw a collection of outdoor equipment. There were snowshoes and skis. Sleds and ropes.

Renata walked straight to the wall of ropes. "Have you climbed before?"

"Yes."

"Grab a harness and the basics. Most of the passageways are level and sloping, but there are a few drops and I don't want us to get stuck. Some of the passages are narrow. You'll have trouble getting through some areas with your shoulders."

Max had a dreadful feeling in the pit of his stomach. "Renata, are you sure this is a good idea?"

"I don't know if there are others with her, but if she's run away, if there is a mother—"

"If there is a mother, there could be an angel." He gripped her shoulders. "Have you thought about that?"

"What are our choices?" She shrugged off his hands and secured her harness before she gathered an armful of ropes. "If there is an angel, then we reassess. I don't sense one. I saw one child, and she was tired and thin. There's a storm out there. She needs our help."

Max didn't try to argue any more. He grabbed the ropes and followed her back to the library. Wading into the twisting passageways had been difficult for Renata when she was steeped in memory. In the face of a rescue, however, she showed no hesitation. She walked to the left corridor and pulled back a tapestry hanging on one wall. There was a narrow passageway behind it and a gust of warm wind.

"This is the only one we left open because it's the main source of heat. This passage leads to the springs," she said. "Can you make it?"

"I'll be fine. Lead the way."

She ducked under the archway and turned sideways. Max followed her, inching along until he felt the tunnel widen. As it widened, the warmth built and he could feel sweat running down his back. The air grew damper and warmer. Max truly understood why the original Irina built here.

"How hot are the springs?"

"I've never taken the temperature," she said. "But I know some of the adults would come and bathe in one, so it can't be too hot."

The tunnel widened into a small room of smooth limestone. Max, headlamp affixed to his forehead, scanned the walls. "This was a ritual room once."

"Probably. The library is far older than the house. In the beginning, they only lived in the caves. The houses came later."

Deep grooves were cut into the walls, the Old Language written in a script long out of fashion. He'd seen an old scribe once with script like this, but it had been in Syria decades before. They passed from the ritual room into another tunnel, that one just as steamy.

"We'll pass the first hot spring in the next room."

"Did you come here as a child?"

Renata smiled over her shoulder. "It was strictly forbidden for children to play in the caverns. Of course I did."

He followed her though the tunnel and into the first spring room. It was completely dark, but his headlamp revealed niches along the wall for torches, and a cool gust of air told him there was ventilation built into the cavern. The pool was only a few meters across, and he could see the bottom. The water bubbled up from the shallow depths and ran out over a lip, splashing into the darkness beyond his sight and feeding one of the underground streams that echoed in the distance.

"This is where they bathed," Renata said. "There are vents carved above that keep the air fresh, but they don't let too much of the weather in."

Max saw curls of vapor rising from the pool. "Are any of the gases dangerous?"

"Not that I know of."

Max scanned the room, noting the flat walkway that surrounded the pool. It had to be partly natural and partly magic. There was no other explanation for the smooth benches and even walkways around a hot spring in a mountain cave. This had been a well-loved place and would have been popular for bathing in a time long before modern luxuries like heated baths.

Touching his *talesm prim*, Max brought his magic to life. The darkness grew lighter, his hearing more sensitive. It was a blessing and a curse. Every small drop and drip echoed in the darkness. He could hear small animals—bats probably—flapping their wings. The key was to filter out the background noise and listen for anything out of place.

He closed his eyes and listened for a few minutes, searching the darkness for human sounds.

Gravel scattering across a floor.

"Did you hear that?" he murmured.

"No. Where?"

There were two passageways branching off the spring room. Max pointed to the right one and Renata walked toward it. Just as he approached the tunnel, he paused, noticing something on the ground.

"Renata."

She paused and turned around. Max pointed to the ground where the outline of a footprint was visible. It wasn't just obviously human. It was obviously human and big. Adult sized. There was either a woman with very large feet traveling through the caverns, or there was a man.

Renata nodded and Max saw a mask of grim determination slide over her face. She turned back to the passageway and walked into the darkness.

THE CAVERNS behind Ciasa Fatima were a rabbit warren. They twisted and turned, branching multiple times. Passageways narrowed and widened. There were small rooms and low crawl spaces. If Renata hadn't been leading, Max knew he would have gotten lost. He'd checked with her several times, but she said she was more than familiar with their surroundings and would have no problems finding their way back. Every now and then, she'd point out landmarks that barely seemed visible or notable to Max, but they meant something to her, and she kept walking.

It was past the fourth pool that they found evidence of habitation in a wide hollow in the rock. It was a small room with smooth walls and a makeshift bed in the corner.

Renata crouched down near the pallet and brought a corner up to her nose. "Grass. It smells like the meadow grass from the hills," she said. "It's not that old."

"So whoever is here has been here since before there was snow on the ground."

"Yes."

It was a large mattress, even if it was thin, and there was a stack of makeshift pillows and blankets at the foot. Another stack of books sat near the pallet, and Max could see the ground kicked up and scrapes on the stone floor.

"I think whoever was here had more things," he said. "More luggage."

"They're running?"

"That mattress is large enough for an adult and a child. Maybe two adults." Max looked at Renata, waiting for her to meet his eyes. "Renata, there could be two of them."

The books were a collection of English, Italian, Turkish, and Arabic. Some were only pamphlets. Others were magazines. It was a scattered collection of writing that told Max whoever lived here had traveled from the east and collected things to read as they went. Refugees with a *kareshta* child?

He looked around the room and noticed something in the corner. He crouched down and pointed his headlamp at the painting on the wall. In the darkness, he could see more work from a familiar artist.

The child who had painted the animal pictures in the classroom had also worked on this wall. The crayons didn't work as well on stone, but he could see light outlines of a flat-topped house and a group of trees and play equipment like he'd seen in human parks. There were dogs and cats. A bed with a pink bedspread and dolls lined up beside it.

"Renata, you need to come see this."

She was already back in the passageway. He could hear her footsteps growing fainter as she continued her search.

In the far corner was one last picture, drawn in more detail than the others. A man and woman holding hands. On the man's shoulders perched a little girl holding a purple balloon. The man had a beard and he was smiling. The woman wore a blue head scarf and she was smiling too. She was grasping the man's hand, a spotted dog's leash held in her other hand. Smiles. Ease. Peace. A pink bedroom and a park with swings. A beloved pet and a bright purple balloon.

"They're a family," he whispered. What kind of family had a *kareshta* child?

He looked again at the man and woman holding hands.

A Grigori family, of course.

Max heard Renata's breath catch and echo a second before her feet started to move.

She was running.

Max stood. "Renata!"

As soon as he entered the passageway, he smelled it. The scent of sandalwood was drifting in the air. Sandalwood meant Grigori.

And Grigori meant Renata was on the hunt.

———

HE USED his senses to track her, but it was difficult. Renata had been evading fallen angels, Grigori, and Irin scribes for centuries. She knew these tunnels like the back of her hand. She also had a knee-jerk reaction to Grigori. If she found the man in the pictures, she would stab first and ask questions later, possibly traumatizing the very child she was trying to help.

He came to a halt when the passage dead-ended. Max turned and faced the darkness, knowing he had no hope of catching her before she found the man she was hunting.

"Renata!"

Max walked back down the tunnel, sweeping his headlamp back and forth, trying to hear anything familiar.

"Renata, he is not your enemy." Max couldn't know that for sure, but he was hoping that a man who carried a little girl on his shoulders, bought her a purple balloon, and made her mother smile was not an enemy. Was the mother human or Grigori? The child had too much magic to be only a quarter angelic. "It's a family, Renata. A man and a woman. A little girl." He saw a dark tunnel entrance to the left that he'd missed the first time. he walked through it, hoping that this was the direction she'd gone.

"They lived in a city, Reni. They had a little dog. They went to the park together. He carried her on his shoulders."

Max started running when he heard her. It wasn't Renata, but it was a child. And that child was crying.

He ran full speed down the passageway, using her cries to guide him. He turned right at a fork, hoping that the strange acoustics in the mountain weren't playing tricks on his senses. When the crying grew louder, he ran faster.

He almost missed them in his desperate search. He passed a long section of rock and heard the little girl's breath catch. Backing up slowly, Max crouched down and looked into a crevice.

His headlamp caught a flash of blue. He took off the bright light and shone it at the floor. The woman in the blue head scarf was hiding in the crevice, her amber-gold eyes wide and frightened, her hand pressed over the mouth of the little girl who squinted at the light. Taking a guess, he spoke in Arabic.

"My name is Max." He held out his hand. "I'm not here to hurt you. I promise."

Both the woman's and the little girl's eyes were bright gold. The woman, like the man, was angelic offspring. Was the child their own? The little girl didn't look like the woman. They might have been sisters of the same angelic father, not mother and daughter. It wouldn't be the first time siblings had protected younger children from the Fallen.

"I don't want to hurt you, but I'm afraid my friend thinks the man with you is dangerous."

The woman in the blue head scarf shook her head violently. *No!*

The little girl pried the woman's hand away from her mouth. "*Mama?*"

The woman kept shaking her head. She curled into herself, trying to move farther away from Max.

"He doesn't have knives, Mama."

The woman shook her head again.

"I promise you"—Max looked at the woman—"I promise you I mean you no harm. I know there are Grigori like you. I know you're trying to live quietly. I saw your room. I saw your daughter's paintings."

The woman stared at him but didn't speak.

"You live up here to get away from the voices, don't you? So she won't have them in her head." He nodded at the little girl. "You're a good mother."

Mother, mother, mother. This was a *kareshta* with a magical child. A *kareshta* in the company of a Grigori with a child pointed to one obvious conclusion. "You're a family, aren't you? The man, he's your mate."

The woman frowned but still didn't speak.

"We like it here," the little girl said. "I don't hear anyone up here except Mama and Baba. And sometimes there are a few people in the summer. But they don't bother me too much. They usually have happy thoughts because they're on holiday."

"Is it better in the library?"

"There's magic there," she whispered. "Do you feel it too? It feels so nice."

Max smiled. "I do."

"I like playing in the library." She looked at her mother with guilty eyes. "I'm not supposed to, but I do."

Just like Renata, the little girl had ventured into the forbidden. "I often did things I wasn't allowed to when I was your age."

"Did your mother get angry with you?"

My mother is dead, he thought. *Killed by brothers of the man who fathered you.*

It was all too twisted and heartbreaking to share. The child was an innocent. Looking at the woman, Max knew that she—unlike her daughter—knew the truth. Their races were at war, and if Max didn't find Renata quickly, there might be another casualty that night.

"I'll find them," he told the woman. "Which way did he go?"

The woman pointed to the right.

Max said, "Stay here. Stay hidden. I'll come back for you."

Following the passageway as it sloped down, Max felt the air grow colder and drier. He was leaving the warmth of the hot springs and entering the heart of the mountain. Limestone glittered around him and stalactites glittered from the ceiling above. He paused where the passage branched and listened.

There. Finally.

There was muffled scuffling in the distance and labored breathing. Max ran in the direction of the fight, almost running over Renata as she charged the man holding a silver dagger, crouched across from her in fighting position. Blood marked his cheek and one eye was turning black. Renata's shirt was torn and she was leaning heavily on her left knee.

"Stop!"

"He's Grigori."

"He's a father," Max said, trying to move between Renata and the man she was fighting. "The child we saw? She's his."

The Grigori swept a leg out and tried to trip Max.

"I'm trying to help you!" Max shouted. "Both of you need to listen. Do you want your daughter to be an orphan?"

"She's better off an orphan than under the thumb of a monster like him!" Renata said.

"Will you listen to yourself!" Max shouted, his arms up, still trying to defuse the two combatants. "Renata, this is a father protecting his mate and child. Would you kill him for protecting his child?"

"She's *kareshta*," Renata said. "She's not his."

"I've seen her. Seen the mother. Seen him. The girl looks exactly like him. Her mother may be *kareshta*, but that child isn't *kareshta*.

She's a free Grigori child, born of free Grigori parents. They are not our enemy."

"I am free of my sire." The man's voice came out rough, speaking in heavily accented English. "Thawra is not free. That is part of why we are in hiding."

Max muttered, "Not helping."

Renata had lost the furious rage and looked more confused than murderous. "What are you talking about?"

"I am free," the Grigori said. He kept his knife up, but his posture relaxed incrementally. "My sire, Jaron, is dead. I was living in Damascus when I felt him die."

"But your mate," Max said. "She is not free?"

"No. I agreed to help her brothers for safety in their city. She's the daughter of Melek. Many of her brothers have tried to kill their father, but they have failed."

"Melek's children?" Max asked. "Born to a Yazidi mother then?"

The man nodded. "Melek sells his daughters. He sends all of them away except for his guards. I took her away from the people who bought her. She was in a village, so I brought her to Damascus. She didn't like the city, but she was coping. For some reason, the voices weren't as bad when we were together."

Max felt ancient magic run along his skin when he realized what the man was saying. He looked at Renata and realized that she'd understood as well.

"Because she's your *reshon*," Renata murmured. "Your touch will make the voices go away." She looked stunned. Dazed. She looked between Max and the Grigori, then stepped back and lowered her knives. "Max?"

He shook his head. "I know it seems improbable, but..."

"Are you going to kill me?" the Grigori asked.

Renata's face was blank. "When was the last time you killed a human?"

The man's eyes filled with guilt. "Seventy years. When was the last time you killed a Grigori?"

Renata sheathed her knives. "Ten days."

The man's face went pale. "They need me. I know I'm a murderer, but please don't take me away from them."

Max stepped between Renata and the Grigori. "We can talk about this."

Her eyes were blank and cold. Nevertheless, Max was hopeful. The knives were put away.

Renata jerked her head toward the passageway. "Follow me."

"I can't leave Thawra and Evin in the caves alone."

"We'll pass them on the way back," Max said. He grabbed Renata's hand and knit their fingers together. "Are you ready?"

"No," Renata said. "But I can lead them back to the library. They can shelter there until the weather clears. Then I want them gone."

IT PROBABLY TOOK an hour to get back to the library, twisting and turning through the maze of passages and caverns. Only Evin, the little Grigori girl, and Renata seemed to know the way. Max helped the Grigori, who introduced himself as Zana, and Thawra, his mate, carry the satchels with their clothes and food stores.

"How long have you been in the caverns?" Max asked Zana.

"About two years. We had made a small house in the mountains behind the big house we saw in the meadow. But when the snow came, we started to look for more solid shelter. We worry about Evin most of all. Contact with Thawra keeps her steady, but there's nothing I can do for Evin. If she's around people, she can't block it out. Her hearing is too acute."

Max saw Evin following Renata, staring up at the Irina warrior with wide, awestruck eyes.

"She doesn't know anything," Zana said. "Evin is an innocent. She knows nothing of our world. She didn't even realize she wasn't human when we lived in Damascus. She thought everyone heard the whispers. That's what she called them. 'The whispers.' We lived a quiet, peaceful life for years, but the war reached us when she was five. There was so much horror. The voices of the dying and the grieving. She and Thawra both started to shut down. Then our own home was destroyed. We had to leave. We made it here, but we'll always be in hiding."

"Are you Turkish?" Max said.

"My mother was Kurdish."

Max glanced at Thawra. "And she's Yazidi?"

"Our human blood means nothing to us, but we could be killed anywhere we went if the humans knew where we came from. We couldn't stay in Syria. Turkey is complicated too. Europe seemed like the only option."

"Why Italy?"

"Thawra was studying Italian before the war. She wanted to read Dante in the original language. I can speak nearly anything if I see it written. It seemed like the best place, and it's easy to get lost in the mountains here."

Max asked, "Does she speak?" He watched the thin woman walking behind Renata, her hand clutching her daughter's hand.

"She can. She usually doesn't. She never has as long as I've known her." Sorrow and devotion were written clearly on the man's face. "Sometimes in her sleep she'll talk."

"Was Melek abusive?"

"He's insane." Zana's voice turned hard. "Not abusive. Not exactly. Unlike most of the Fallen, he thinks his daughters are his most precious children. In the past, he would sell them to various tribes as prophets and seers. He doesn't understand that the world doesn't work that way anymore. Most people don't believe in prophets and seers. When he sold his children to modern humans..."

Heaven above. They'd put Melek's daughters in asylums. Burn them as witches. Or worse. Zana had mentioned Thawra being sold, but Max didn't want to pry.

"We'll get you help," Max said. "I don't know how, but we'll figure something out."

As far as Max knew, no other Irin had encountered what Thawra, Zana, and Evin were: a true Grigori family. Thawra and Zana were mated, though it was doubtful any kind of ceremony had taken place. Evin was born from their union. A child of half-human and half-angelic blood, the same as the Irin. She was a second-generation Grigori child. Her powers would be formidable and possibly different from anything they'd known. Closer to the odd powers Ava and Malachi's children were exhibiting than anything they'd encountered before.

Whatever they were, Max wanted to help them. He recognized someone who was searching for a home.

CHAPTER NINE

Renata lay on the bed, listening to the bustle of activity below. Max was being charming with the child, making her laugh and playing the guitar for her. He'd fed the family and found more blankets and sleeping bags for them, building a comfortable resting place in the library where her people had been slaughtered.

What are you doing to me, Maxim?

Renata felt like a monster, but she couldn't be near them. Even the voice of the male made her ill. The smell of sandalwood in her house drove her mad. As soon as the small family left, she'd have to open all the windows to rid the house of the scent or risk going crazy.

She heard someone on the stairs and sat bolt upright in bed. Luckily, after a few seconds she recognized Max's step.

He poked his head in the doorway. "How are you?"

She shook her head and motioned him in. "Close the door, please."

Max did, then came to the bed, crawling next to her and wrapping her in his arms.

"I can't imagine what you're feeling," he said. "So I'm not going to say I understand. But thank you for letting them stay."

"I'm not going to send a child into a storm," she said. "Not going to send a helpless woman out there either."

"But the man?"

"If he were alone, he'd already be dead."

Max squeezed her tighter. "You realize he's Ava's uncle. In a sense."

"She doesn't know him. She'd never feel the loss."

"Does that make it right?"

"For the women he killed in the past? Yes. For the humans he preyed on before he found a conscience? Yes, killing him seems right."

Max didn't say anything. "Part of me knows you're right. Part of me knows that murder is murder. And we can't forget that."

"And the other part of you?"

"The other part of me remembers Kostas. Sees this man, Zana. Recognizes the struggles free Grigori have willingly taken on to fight against their own nature when they have fathers who encourage them to plunder this world."

"To plunder us," she whispered.

"Zana was not alive during the Rending. Few Grigori who are living now were."

Renata's throat was tight. Tears stung her eyes. "I tell myself that over and over, Max. But every time I smell their scent, I'm right back in the library, grasping at hollow clothes and empty blankets where the babies were. They killed our mothers. Killed babies in their cradles. Killed more than warriors. They killed the innocent."

"I know."

"They killed those who were running. Killed my parents who only wanted to create beautiful things and sing songs and debate arcane academic points with other scholars. They killed Balien, who was only trying to protect others." She turned around to face him. "They killed your mother. Your aunt. Your father. They might as well have killed your uncle and your grandfather too. Our people were cut in half. Thrown into chaos."

Max smoothed her hair back from her forehead. "I know. But not by him. Not by Zana."

"By others like him."

"And many of the same people hunt him now. Hunt his mate and child." Max squeezed his eyes shut. "There are no easy answers, Renata. When do we forgive the children of our murderers? When do we let go?"

She felt the hot tears slip down her cheek. "I don't know if I can."

He said nothing, but he didn't turn away in disgust or disappointment. He held her closer and kissed her forehead. He kissed the tears from her cheeks and rocked her back and forth as she cried silently.

"You're a better person than me," she said.

"No. I just don't remember my loss as keenly as you do. I was a child."

Renata said nothing, but she didn't agree. Max was a better person than her. He'd lost his mother and his father before he could even remember them. He'd been raised in a world devoid of art and beauty and fine things. He'd grown up in a world were kindness was a luxury and gentleness a weakness.

And yet he didn't turn away from the most vulnerable. He chose to use his strength and the harsh reality of his own past to create a safe place for those who needed it, even if they were the blood of his enemies.

Renata took a deep breath and lifted her head from his chest. "Did you need something from me?"

"I only wanted to check on you." He played with her hair. "I can bring some food up if you don't want to come downstairs."

"I'm not a coward," she said. "I just... I don't want to let that girl see how I react to her father. It's not her fault, and she loves him."

"She's a darling child," Max said. "She's safe and secure. Obviously loved. She's bright and funny. You can tell she feels very safe here."

Renata smiled a little. "Her home was in the caverns, so she snuck into the library. My home was in the library, so I snuck into the caverns."

"Both of you little rule-breakers. Probably driving your poor mothers crazy."

Mothers.

"Thawra," Renata said. "The *kareshta* woman."

"What about her?" Max asked.

"She has no shields."

"No." He cleared his throat. "I actually thought about that, but since she refuses to talk—Zana says she's never spoken willingly as long as he's known her, and that's over fifteen years—I don't think shields would be effective. She has to use her voice to make magic, doesn't she?"

"Yes."

Max shook his head. "I don't think she would."

"Would she for her child?"

Max frowned.

"There are spells," Renata said. "Spells to protect your daughter from the voices."

"But Evin is old enough to learn her own shielding."

"And if her mother refuses to shield her, I'll teach her those spells. But if Thawra thinks that the only way she can protect her daughter is with her voice, then I'm betting she'll use it. And if she uses it for her daughter, she can use it for herself too. And if she uses it for herself, then she'll know that she has power."

For some reason, giving Thawra power felt important. That was something her mother would be proud of. That was something Renata could do. She couldn't bring back her family, but she could help this mother and her child.

She could at least do that.

MAX KEPT Zana out in the yard, chopping firewood with him while Renata went to the library. As she entered, she heard Evin giggle. Thawra was building a fort from the blankets and the furniture left in the library, using odds and ends to hold the blankets in place as Evin rolled under them in the red sleeping bag Max had given them.

"Are you and Baba going to sleep down here with me?"

Thawra signed, and Renata was surprised and pleased that the woman used British Sign Language, the same as her sister Mala used.

We'll sleep in our own bed, little bug.

"But why? There's room here," Evin whined. "I want us to be all together."

We are always together. Maybe Baba wants a rest from your kicks at night, huh? Thawra smiled.

"I do not kick Baba!"

You do. You kick me too.

"Are you going to tell the nice man about the new baby?"

Renata must have made sound of surprise, because Thawra and Evin both turned toward her.

"You're pregnant?" Renata asked.

Thawra looked frightened, and Evin quickly scrambled out of the blanket fort and over to Renata.

"I was just pretending," the little girl said. "I was just—"

Thawra clapped and brought Evin to attention.

Don't lie, she signed. *Especially to those offering shelter to us. Let me and Baba deal with this.*

"Mama, I'm sorry."

Thawra's whole face softened. *Little bug, don't be sorry. I'm happy you're excited about the baby.*

"Babies are exciting things," Renata said quietly. "I'm sure you'll be an excellent big sister."

No wonder the Grigori had fought so fiercely. He wasn't only protecting his child, he was also protecting a pregnant mate. Irin men were known to be more than a bit wild and overprotective when their mates were pregnant.

Apparently Grigori men were the same.

You understand sign, Thawra asked.

"I have a sister who lost her voice during the Rending," Renata said. "She uses the same sign language you use."

Zana taught me when we were first together, Thawra said. *Before that, I had no speech, though I could read and write a little.*

"And Mama and Baba taught me!" Evin, sensing she wasn't in trouble, had climbed on the back of a sofa. "That was my first language, wasn't it Mama?"

Yes, little bug.

"But now I speak sign and Arabic, and English, and I'm learning Italian."

Renata walked over as Thawra tried to get Evin down off the furniture. "You must be very smart."

"I am. My Baba says I am a clever, clever girl."

Thawra's eyes were wary and worried as Renata drew closer.

"I'm not going to harm you or your family," she said.

Zana says that we must leave after the storm passes. We have nowhere else to go.

Renata sighed. "If you think that's actually going to happen, you clearly don't understand Max at all."

Evin bounced over and sat by Renata. "I like Max."

"I do too." She tucked Evin's hair behind her ear. "You remind me very much of myself when I was your age. Do you know I lived here when I was a girl?"

"You did?" Evin grinned. "Did you sleep in the caves like me?"

Renata felt the pang of guilt, but since the child clearly felt like sleeping in the library was an adventure, she tried not to feel too guilty.

"No, I slept in the house. I had a room there with my parents.

There were many families here, and my parents worked here in the library with many people. Clever people like you, who knew lots of languages and stories. I went to school here."

Evin's face fell a little. "I can't go to school."

Renata looked at Thawra. "What if I told you there was magic you could use to help her block out the voices?"

What kind of magic?

"Irina magic."

Thawra's eyes went wide. *The singers?*

"Have you met any of our kind before?"

She shook her head. *Only stories.*

"You have angel blood. That means you have the same magic we do. Irina mothers use magic to protect their children when they're young. You could use the same magic to protect Evin from the soul voices—your other child too, if it's a girl—but you'd have to speak."

Thawra eyes were blank.

"Mama doesn't talk." Evin leaned closer to Renata and whispered, "The bad people hurt her heart. That's what Baba says. That's why she doesn't talk except for bad dreams. Baba and me sleep by her at night and hug her lots if she cries."

Thawra clapped sharply. *Evin, that's enough.*

The bad people hurt her heart. Renata wondered if Thawra's natural magic had something to do with empathy. If she were Irina, Renata would say she carried the angel Chamuel's blood. Those of Chamuel's blood were unusually empathetic. Some could even heal emotional injuries to others. Conversely, they were some of the most traumatized Irina during the Rending. They lived not only through their own trauma, but also through the trauma of those around them.

They had to leave Syria, Max had said. *Zana said they were shutting down.*

"You're an empath," Renata said, trying to catch Thawra's eye. "You feel what others feel."

So does Evin, Thawra signed.

"I can teach you magic to protect yourself. To protect her. You'd be able to be around humans. You'd be able to live a more normal life."

Thawra shook her head. *We have no papers. We are nobody. Nothing.*

"Don't say that, Mama." Evin hopped off the sofa and went to her mother, wrapping her arms around Thawra's hips. "Baba says you are his moon. *Ya amar,* Mama. *Ya habib alby.* And I am his ladybug."

Thawra took a deep breath and stroked Evin's hair back. *Go see the Christmas tree,* she signed. *Let me talk to the lady.*

"Go ahead," Renata said. "When Max comes in, ask him for a biscuit. There are some in the kitchen. I made them with dried apricots."

"I like biscuits!" Evin bounced away through the stone hallway and past the iron door that hung open, leading to the house.

Renata turned back to Thawra. "You don't want her to hear you speak, do you?"

Thawra opened her mouth and breathed deeply for a very long time. Then she put a hand on her belly and pushed out the words. "My voice. Sounds like a child."

It did sound childlike. It was high and scratched. Something about it reminded Renata of a cat mewling.

"How old were you when you stopped speaking?"

"Younger," she rasped. *Younger than Evin,* she signed.

"Why?"

"Mad," she said.

"You were mad? Angry?"

Thawra shook her head. "The family... sold—" *The family I was sold to,* she signed. *They told me my voice was driving them mad. Anytime I opened my mouth, they beat me. So I stopped speaking. It was safer that way.*

111

Renata's fury was ripe and fresh. "Your voice is a gift. We are daughters of the Creator. Our voices sing the songs of heaven. Those people were ignorant fools who knew nothing of your power. *Nothing.* Do you hear me? Your voice is power, and I will teach you how to use it. To protect yourself. To protect your children." Renata took a deep breath. "And to calm and strengthen the mate who protects you."

Thawra's golden eyes met Renata's. "I have… magic?"

Renata's mind drifted back to a cold stone church, lying on the hard marble—empty and grieving—as a woman far more powerful than she'd been held out a hand to her.

"Can you teach me to be a warrior?"
"Can you heal my wound?"

"You have more magic than you know," Renata said. "And I can teach you to use it. I can teach you how to fight."

Thawra's chin lifted, and Renata no longer saw a frightened victim. She saw a woman who hoped.

Hope was powerful.

"I will learn," Thawra rasped out. "I want to."

Renata held her hand out to Thawra. "Then you are exactly where you need to be."

RENATA WATCHED the family that night at dinner. Max had made a stew he'd learned from his uncle, a typical warrior's meal with boiled meat and potatoes and root vegetables. It was perfect for dinner, and the little family wolfed it down. Renata had peeked at their stores. They'd been existing on canned meats and beans and flour they'd probably scavenged from the house. Though all of them were thinner than they ought to have been, Zana was nearly gaunt. It was obvious he'd been going without food so Thawra and

Evin could eat.

"What did you do?" Renata asked quietly as they were finishing their food. It was the first time she'd spoken to Zana since she'd called him a monster and tried to kill him. "Before the war. Back in Damascus. What was your profession?"

He smiled a little. "I was a carpenter. I worked for myself, which let me avoid most people."

Grigori, like Irin scribes, could not sustain contact with humans without draining them of their life force. But while Irin scribes had magic to help their control, Grigori were given no such knowledge by their angelic fathers.

"Did you do some work on the porch?" Max asked casually. "Over on the east side? I noticed some of the wood was different."

"I did," Zana said. "I found some lumber in the barn last summer and decided to replace a few of the railings." He glanced at Renata warily. "I didn't think anyone would mind. They were loose. I didn't want anyone to fall. And we'd taken some food from storage in the house."

"It's fine," Renata said absently. "Thank you for fixing it."

"You're most welcome." Zana reached over and used his napkin to wipe Evin's cheek. "Drink all your milk, bug."

"It tastes funny," Evin whispered.

"It's different because it's fresh," Zana said. "But fresh is better. It will make you strong."

Max reached for Renata's hand under the table.

Thawra tapped the table and signed, *Zana is very gifted. He was more than a carpenter. He was an artist. He sold a table for one hundred forty thousand pounds once.*

"What was that?" Max asked. Renata translated for him.

Zana laughed ruefully. "It's a good thing I changed our money to gold. That much in Syrian pounds wouldn't even buy the lumber for that table anymore."

Max asked, "Where you able to bring some money out?"

Zana nodded. "I have some savings. I always kept gold. I've lived too long not to know how quickly things can change. But we have no papers, and I'm sure any gold I exchange would not be the correct value on the... informal market. So I've tried to save as much as possible."

Max glanced at Renata. "I think we can help fix the papers situation."

She nodded. "Max is very good at that. Scribes need new papers regularly for brothers who have outlived their current documents."

Thawra and Zana's eyes went wide. "What?" he asked. "You can get us papers?"

"I'll give you Austrian citizenship," Max said. "They're an EU country, so you'll have options. I have plenty of connections in Vienna that can help. And health insurance cards, of course."

Thawra slapped a hand over her mouth but couldn't stop the choking gasp that came from her throat. Tears of relief fell from her eyes and she started to shake.

Evin cried, "Mama, what's wrong?"

Zana threw his arms around his mate. "Thawra, shhh." He looked at Max with fierce eyes. "I can pay you."

"You don't need to pay him," Renata said. "Your family needs help. We can't solve the problems of the whole world, but we can do this. With papers, you'll be able to find work. Carpentry is a skilled trade. You can get Evin in school. Thawra can have proper health care for her and the baby."

Max squeezed her hand. "Save your money, Zana. This is simply the decent thing to do."

Renata noticed Evin close her eyes and press her fingers to her temples. Her little face was scrunched up.

Poor thing.

Not only hearing voices, but also the emotions of those around her. No child should have to sort through the complex emotional maze in the kitchen. Renata rose and held out her hand.

"Evin, come with me for a moment, will you?"

Zana asked, "Where—?"

"Don't worry. I am going to teach her a simple shielding spell I learned at her age. One little song. It will help with the voices. It might also help shield her from emotional waves. I don't know for sure as I'm not an empath, but we can try."

Evin's small forehead was furrowed. "What's an empath? I don't know that word."

Thawra signed, *Are you sure?*

"About the voices? Yes. It's very simple. I'll work on more complex spells for you and the baby later. But for now, I can teach her a children's song that will help with the voices. The emotional shielding, I'm not sure about, but I'll look."

It was past time she refreshed herself and delved into the well of memory she'd spent half her life developing. She knew there were spells she'd learned for Chamuel's daughters. That was part of an archivist's job. She just had to find the trigger to remember them.

Renata led Evin back to the library and sat next to her on the couch.

"Okay, I'm going to teach you a little song, and I want you to sing it just like I do. It has to be exact. Do you think you can do that?"

Evin nodded. "I'm very clever."

Renata smiled. "I know you are."

Even reached out and took her hand. "You're loud."

Renata blinked. "What?"

"You're very loud. You have…" Evin squeezed Renata's hand and sucked in a breath. In a heartbeat, her little face crumpled. "They hurt your heart too," she said as tears ran down her face. "Like Mama. They hurt your heart too."

Evin's small hand clutched hers, and Renata was torn between pulling back and comforting the child, who had started to sob. A moment of hesitation and Renata pulled Evin into her arms, wrapping herself around the little girl who cried as if her heart was breaking.

"Pull back, Evin. Do you know how to pull back?"

Evin pressed her cheek to Renata's and whispered, "I'm sorry."

Renata gasped as the pain struck her chest. Without thought or will, the past rose up and stabbed her, sucking her into a howling storm of memory as the child clutched her neck.

There was laughter and the smell of cinnamon and pine.

Lights and singing.

Then the screaming came.

Her mother's gut-wrenching sobs.

"The children! Renata, where are the children?"

Wails and the sickening scent of sandalwood and blood. Her father's groan of anguish.

"It can't be. It can't be. No, it cannot be."
   "We were gone." Balien's hollow voice. *"I left them. I left them alone."*

Her father's soul.

Silent.

Her mother's soul.

Silent.

The last roar of her lover's voice.

"Renata, you must run!"

Then silence.

Silence.

Silence.

Silence.

Let me die. I do not want to live. Let me die with them. Let me die and go to them. Give me peace.

A sickening whisper in her mind. "There is no peace now."

Renata felt the scream rip from her chest as raw sorrow sprang from her mind and into the dusty air of the library. In the distance, she heard running steps and could only think of Grigori running up the stairs. She fell to the ground and felt the little girl crouch beside her.

"I'm sorry," the little girl whispered again. "I'm sorry."

CHAPTER TEN

Max burst into the library and came to a halt, not understanding what he was seeing before him. He'd heard the child crying. Heard Renata's screams.

His lover was writhing on the ground, curled into the fetal position as the little girl knelt beside her. Evin had her hands on Renata's cheeks, and tears poured down her face, which was set in grim determination. The child looked up as soon as Max and Zana ran in.

"Evin, what are you doing?" Zana yelled at his daughter.

Max knelt and lifted Renata in his arms, but Evin kept her hands on Renata's cheeks.

"The sick"—she sniffed through her tears—"it had to come out. Her heart was hurt."

Empath. Max could see the little girl's skin growing pale even as her golden eyes glowed brighter and brighter.

He said, "Evin, her hurt is too much. You need to stop."

"No." She shook her head. "I can make it better. Someone has to make it better."

Max heard someone else come in the library, but he couldn't turn from Evin's eyes.

"Let her go." It was a woman's voice, rasping and unused. "Evin, let go."

The little girl shook her head. Max held Renata in one arm and gently took Evin's small hand from Renata's skin.

"Let go, little one," he said. "She's lighter now. Can't you feel it?" Maxim did. The spiked energy that always emanated from Renata had softened under the little empath's hand.

Thawra came and knelt by Evin, pulling the child into her embrace and pressing Evin's face to her neck. "Shhhhh." The mother made some sign at Zana, and the Grigori took off down the hall.

Renata was unconscious, her body limp and heavy. He could feel the glow of her magic resting within her, and for the first time in a long time it felt... tired. Not extinguished, but dimmer. He lifted her and sat on the sofa, pressing kisses to her forehead and writing spells on her forehead.

Peace. Hope. Love.

He wrote those simple spells in the Old Language over and over across her forehead.

Peace. Hope. Love.

Max couldn't think of anything more elaborate than that.

Peace. Hope. Love.

Finally, she let out a ragged breath and curled into him.

"Rest, my love." He held Renata and looked to Thawra and Evin. The little girl was limp and drawn, far paler than she should be. "What does she need?"

"These," Zana said from the hallway. He was carrying...

"Is that a box of crayons?"

He set them on the ground beside Thawra and took Evin from her arms. Shoving aside the woven rug on the library floor, he took a crayon from the box, shoved it into Evin's hand and laid her gently on the ground.

"Draw it out, ladybug."

"No paper," Evin whispered.

"Draw on the ground." Zana smoothed back her hair. "Don't worry. It's a strong mountain. It can take the memories."

Thawra lay beside her daughter and held her from behind as Evin's small hand began to move.

Was this how Evin exorcized the emotions she took from others? Max watched in wonder as the black crayon began to move across the plaster-covered floor. He couldn't take his eyes away as angry black lines raked back and forth. Slashes and swirls of black, the crayon pressed so hard it broke in Evin's hand. Zana didn't flinch, he simply handed her another crayon, this one in charcoal grey.

Color touched her cheeks as the picture began to form.

Evin propped herself up on one arm. Then two. She reached for another crayon.

Deep blue joined the swirls of grey and black.

Amethyst purple to deepen the night sky.

Thawra and Zana backed away as Evin regained strength. The little girl crawled across the floor, entirely focused on the picture forming beneath her. Zana held his arms out and Thawra went to him. They sat on the ground, their back against the sofa, watching their daughter create a dark masterpiece on the ground.

Deep umber slopes beneath a jewel-toned sky. Black swirled with grey swirled with white. Evin glanced over her shoulder at Max and reached for the dark green, leaning close and concentrating on the drawing that took shape on the ground. The little girl leaned back and nodded. Then she bent down again and scraped at something with her fingernail. Reached for the gold. The silver crayon. The grey again. She added details with all the furrowed concentration of a master.

By the time she finished, her face had lost the drawn appearance and only appeared tired.

Zana went to his daughter. "Enough?"

Evin nodded silently.

"Take her in the living room," Max said softly. "I'll bring Renata up to her bedroom in a minute, but I want everyone in the house. It's too cold in here."

Zana nodded and lifted Evin in his arms. The little girl wrapped her arms around her father and laid her head on his shoulder. Her bright gold eyes locked with Max's.

"She'll be better now."

"Thank you, Evin."

He had a feeling Renata would be having a conversation with Zana and Thawra as soon as she woke. A young empath could easily hurt herself by taking on too great a sorrow, and Renata's sorrow was incredibly deep.

Max stood and finally saw the drawing that Evin had created on the floor of the library.

She'd drawn a mountain that rose high among a rolling range of snow-covered peaks. The deep blue and purple sky was clear and studded with bright gold stars where the little girl's fingernail had scraped away the darkest colors. The storm Evin drew swirled around the slopes of the mountain, as violent as the howling wind outside. Black and grey joined by silver-toned ice that beat and battered the angled heights.

But though the storm swept the slopes, the bottom of the mountain sat wide and sure in a valley bathed in moonlight. Deep green trees covered the mountain, partly shielding it from bitter wind.

The mountain rose in the night sky, steady and unmoved despite the violent storm that battered it.

Oh, my love. Max kissed Renata's forehead. *Your strength humbles me.*

He walked around Evin's drawing and back into the house. Zana and Thawra were arranging blankets and pillows under the tree for Evin, who smiled into the rafters, pointing at the brightly colored stars decorating the ceiling. Thawra and Zana hovered over her, making their own bed near the fire. Max could hear the wind battering the old house, but nothing creaked or moaned. It was as steady as the mountain it rested on, rooted in the love and magic that had built it.

Max walked up the stairs and into their bedroom, shutting the door behind him.

———

HE WOKE to the feel of soft lips pressing kisses to his chest. Max opened his eyes and saw Renata, bright-eyed with a mischievous smile curving her lips.

"Shhhhh." She nodded toward the door. "We still have company."

There were no shadows in her eyes. No worry marring her forehead. She slid up Max's body, wearing nothing but her skin, and took his mouth, luxuriating in his sleepy kiss as she shoved his pants down his hips.

"Naked," she murmured against his lips. "I want you naked."

"Yes." He bit her lower lip and sucked it into his mouth. "I'm getting that."

He rolled to the side and kicked off his pants, running a hand down her back and over her bottom before he hitched her muscled thigh over his own to open her. He was already hard and aching, but all he had to do was catch her scent for that to happen. What heated his blood that morning was the lightness in her eyes.

Renata smiled against his lips and hummed happily as Max slid into her. She curled her leg around his hips and rocked in an easy, sleepy rhythm as they made love in the cozy warmth of their room.

"I love you," he whispered.

"Happy Midwinter." Her eyes sparkled. "I thought this was a good start to the day."

"This is the best start to any day." He voice was rough. "I want to wake up with you every day."

She bit his chin. "How about *most* days?"

A grumble.

"And," she said, "on the nights we aren't together, I will dream-walk by your side. We'll meet each other in our sleep and love each other there, even when we're miles apart, my love."

His heart was so full he couldn't bear it. Dream walking was a special magic reserved for mates. Only mated scribes and singers had the ability to meet each other in dreams, their souls touching even if their bodies were apart. He rolled Renata to her back and sank into her, their easy pace forgotten. He needed her. Needed her laughter and her heat and the brightness in her eyes. Needed the peace of her presence and the comfort of her hand.

"You are my mate," he said, taking her mouth in a hard kiss. "You are my mate, Renata of Fatima."

Her lips were flushed with pleasure, swollen from his kisses. Her breath came in quiet pants as he drove her body to climax.

"You are my mate, Maxim of Riga," she breathed out. "I will have no other."

"I will have no other." He heard the quiet catch of her breath. "I want no other but you. Forever."

Her body tightened around him, and her back arched in pleasure when she came. Max drove into her, biting the pillow beside her instead of shouting his pleasure when he climaxed. He let out a long breath and fell to the side, gathering Renata to his arms, locking their bodies together.

"I want to stay in bed all day," he said.

"We have guests."

Somewhere below them, the smell of baking bread and the sound of bright voices drifted up the stairs.

"Hang our guests," Max said. "They know where the food is."

Renata ran her fingers through his short hair. "Is Evin well?"

He nodded. "What did she do?"

"It felt like someone lancing an infection," Renata said. "It all poured out. And it hurt. So, so badly."

He hugged her closer.

"But then it was gone. And... I don't know. Things feel clearer.

The pool is still filled with water, but she cleaned out the leaves and muck that had fallen in. I can see the bottom now."

Max kissed her forehead. "I'm glad."

"You know we can't really hide in bed all day, right?"

He lifted his head. "There's a washbasin in the corner. We've made do with worse amenities over the years."

She laughed, truly laughed, and he fell in love with her all over again.

"We can't stay in bed all day," she said. "Today is Midwinter. And there's a little girl downstairs who deserves to celebrate."

THAT NIGHT RENATA helped Evin light the Midwinter candles, the sweet smell of beeswax filling the dining room where their feast was laid out. Combining their food stores had led to a far more luxurious meal than Max had expected.

They had a roast from Zana's frozen store of winter venison he'd hunted before the storm and roasted potatoes Renata had brought from the village. She'd also brought mild red sauerkraut and a cabbage salad with carrots. Thawra had taught Renata how to make soft sweet rolls she called *kulicha*, filled with dates and hazelnuts, and a chickpea stew simmered in spicy tomatoes and chilies.

Evin had stuffed herself with so many sweets Max didn't know how she ate anything once they sat down, but Zana filled her plate and she ate everything but the sauerkraut, chattering away about the songs Renata had taught her that day and the newfound silence in her mind.

And though Renata still sat at the opposite end of the table from Zana, she smiled and asked him more questions about his life and business in Syria. She told him she had a sister with Jaron's blood and sat silently as Max told them the story of Jaron's fall and hopeful redemption. Max could tell the story moved both Zana and Thawra greatly.

After dinner, Max got out the guitar to play some Midwinter music, and Renata surprised him again by singing a traditional song in the style of the Southern Alps, her voice lighter and more playful than he'd ever heard in his life. He watched her as she sang, imagining the living room filled with their own family, imagining friends who came to visit this house, filling it with love and laughter and new memories.

He wanted it desperately.

Renata met his eyes, smiling as she sang one song after another. In the music, he heard her heart waking.

She would always be a warrior. Always.

Perhaps if life had not turned the way it had, she wouldn't have been. Perhaps she would have been a scholar and a mother and a mate, passing on her songs to other singers and living out her life with another man.

But the storm had come, and it had not been gentle. The scars had broken the path of her life, cutting off some trails even as it cleared others. In another life, Max might never have known her, might never have loved her.

Did that make him thankful for the storm?

No. He simply accepted it.

Max set the guitar down and joined Renata on the sofa when they were finished singing. Thawra had taken a mandolin from the music room and tuned it. She started playing on it, picking through the notes carefully until she became accustomed to the instrument.

"It's very like a *tambur*," Zana said. "Not exactly, but it's close."

"And she plays?" Renata asked.

"She plays beautifully." The love on the man's face was so evident Max almost looked away. "Her mother taught her before she died, and Thawra has already started teaching Evin."

Evin was sitting at her mother's feet, watching everything Thawra did with unwavering attention.

"Your daughter is extremely bright," Renata said.

Zana put a hand over his heart and bowed his head. "Thank you. She is a gift to us."

"She picked up the simple magic I taught her today almost instantly."

Max said, "She reminds me of Matti."

Renata nodded. "I had the same thought."

"Who is Matti?" Zana asked.

"My brother's child," Max said. "She has two different fallen archangels in her bloodline, so Matti and her brother are... different. We think. But Ava and Malachi seem well prepared in dealing with them."

"We have no idea what to do with her magic," Zana said. "Thawra does her best to understand, but her abilities are quite different than Evin's. She can feel emotions very strongly, but she doesn't drain them from others the way Evin does."

"She might be able to if she's trained in more magic," Renata said as Thawra started playing a lively tune by the fire.

"Perhaps," Zana said. "The only solution so far has been to isolate them. That's why we liked this mountain. The village is close enough for me to visit for supplies, but the caves are isolated enough to keep them from being overwhelmed."

Max watched Renata, wondering if her mind was going where his was.

"You should stay," she said quietly.

Zana was wary. "I know something very upsetting happened here. I can guess some things. I know this is your home. We do not want to disrespect your home in any way."

"The school in the village is good." Renata ignored his objections. "It's a long walk, but it's possible."

Max put a hand on the back of her neck. "Renata, are you sure?"

She took a deep breath and turned to Zana. "I am uncomfortable with you. That is not your fault. It simply is."

Zana nodded but didn't say a word.

"But I respect what you have done to protect your mate and

126

child," she continued. "And your daughter..." Renata cleared her throat. "She healed a very deep wound in me. One that I did not think would ever leave me. I am not healed entirely, but I will be one day. And I have Evin to thank for that."

Zana said, "There is no debt."

"It's not a debt I object to," Renata said. "You're right. This is a safe place. It's also a good one. There was a garden here once. There was a dairy that produced the sweetest milk I've ever tasted. This was a safe place for travelers and those seeking shelter."

Max squeezed her hand. "There is a cottage beside the dairy barn."

"It could be repaired," Renata said. "You could live here and make this place a haven again. You could take care of guests and fix things. You know how to do that."

Zana nodded, and Max could see the man's eyes shining. "I am good at fixing things. And Thawra is an excellent gardener. I have never kept cows, but I grew up with goats."

Renata laughed and blinked hard. "Goats would work too."

"Renata—"

"I think you found this place for a reason," she said in a rush. "I think your family came here for a reason. Your steps were guided by heaven, and we should honor that. Stay here, Zana. Raise your children here. Max and I can help you."

"And you would be a help to us," Max added. "I know this place would be well tended in your and Thawra's care."

Renata said, "And there are songs I should teach Evin. She has the gift of memory. She can learn the songs."

The music had stopped, and Max glanced over at Thawra and Evin. Thawra had a hand on her chest and eyes that stared at Renata with wary hope.

"Make this your home," Renata said to her. "This was a home for so many for generations. It wants the presence of children again. I can't be here all the time, but if you make this place your home... I would be very happy about that."

Evin's small mouth was hanging open. "Can we stay?"

"You would have to walk a long way to school," Max said, "and help your mother and father."

The little girl nodded. "I can do that." She turned to her mother. "Mama, I can do that."

Thawra started crying. She put a hand to her throat and forced out the words, "Can you teach me… to sing?"

Renata nodded, and Max put his arm around her shoulders.

"Yes," she said. "I can teach you to sing."

CHAPTER ELEVEN

Six months later...

"Where did you send them?" Renata asked as they reached the crest of the hill.

"Cappadocia," Max said.

They'd handed off the car in the village. Zana and Thawra would be taking it for the summer while Max and Renata stayed at Ciasa Fatima.

"Cappadocia?" asked Renata. "Not Istanbul?"

"It was a popular decision. Evin is finished with her first school term. Orsala wanted to work more closely with Thawra, and the brothers in the library there heard we had the world's best carpenter in our employ. They built an addition on the library and need bookcases to fit the caves. They were willing to pay handsomely for the work, so it seemed like perfect timing."

"And Thawra can have the baby surrounded by Irina healers," Renata said. "That will make the birth more comfortable."

"And the scribes can teach Zana the spells he'll need for the child. So you see? A summer in Cappadocia will be warm but will suit everyone." He put an arm around her waist and pulled her close. "Particularly me."

Renata smiled and kissed him. "I'm just glad Zana hasn't bought goats yet."

"Chickens are the only things we have to keep alive. And the vegetable garden."

"So you're going to be a farmer for the summer?"

He raised his eyebrows. "I'm always up for a challenge."

"You better be with a mate like me." She ducked under his arm and raced across the meadow, leaping over the new fences that Zana had built and up onto the porch that no longer creaked.

Max tackled her just as she got the door open. He threw her over his shoulder and dropped his backpack.

"The chickens can wait." He slapped her backside. "I need to claim my woman."

"You know, it's a good thing I packed my knives away, or I'd carve my mating vow into your ass." She slapped it for emphasis, but she was lying. She would never mar Maxim's ass. It would be a crime against heaven.

"You'd never do it," Max said as they walked up the stairs. "You like it too much."

The house smelled of lemon oil and pine. Thawra would have aired it out and made it ready for them before they left. There were flowers in their bedroom, and the windows let in the clear mountain air.

Max set her down and stood staring over her shoulder with his mouth agape. "Heaven above."

"What?" Renata turned from the windows and noticed the bed.

It was a work of art. The formerly rustic wooden bed had been carved with an intricate pattern of stars and flowers. Shining mother-of-pearl inlay decorated each star, the flowers were brightly painted, and darker woods were mixed into the pattern, giving the entire headboard stunning dimension. It was clearly inspired by Syrian design, but the flowers carved into the lattice were the bright yellow, purple, and orange flowers that grew in the meadow in front of the house.

"Oh, Maxim."

"What a gift he has," Max said. "And what a mating gift for us."

Renata smiled. "If you ruin this bed, Maxim, I will never forgive you."

He huffed. "That was a hotel bed in Copenhagen, and I can't believe you're still bringing it up."

"Still." She walked over and dragged him to the new sofa by the window. "Maybe we better start on a slightly less valuable piece of furniture."

"If you insist." Max dragged Renata's shirt over her head and tossed it out the open window. "You won't be needing that for the next few weeks."

"What if I get cold?" The mountain air hit her skin, but she could never be cold looking at Max naked.

As he was becoming. As quickly as possible.

"I'll warm you up," he said. "What are mates for?"

RENATA CLOSED her eyes and gave in to the poetry of his brush on her skin. The dark henna started at the nape of her neck and traveled down her spine, spells her body would capture and hold on to as Maxim made his vow. She sat in the flicker of firelight, cross-legged in the house where she'd been born, waiting for her mate to finish the magic that would tie them together.

"*I searched through the storm,*" he said in a low voice, "*and I found you.*

> "*My beloved is a fox on the mountainside.*
> "*She ran from me until I whispered gently.*"

Renata angled her neck as the sable brush traced over her

shoulder and down her arm. He wrote his spells in the Old Language, the language of heaven and the angels. The language she would sing as they made love.

> *Come, my beloved*
> *Come to my hand*
> *Come to my bed*
> *My Renata, born in love*
> *Born again in blood.*
> *I will ever be your cleft in the rock.*
> *Ever your faithful shelter*
> *Ever and always the blade in your sure hand."*

Max finished the mating mark over her heart, writing the words of his vow where they would glow as the two of them made love. He knelt before her and kissed her lips, careful not to mar any of his work before the ink dried. "I love you, Renata of Fatima."

The air around them was heady with magic. He had marked his vow on her body as he would mark her own vow on his, using the sacred ivory needle to tattoo her promise over his heart. Every moment of passion would become a reminder of their pledge. Every time their magic rose, they would be linked.

Renata closed her eyes and let her head fall back in pleasure. She felt Max all around her, not only in his brush, but his scent and his magic. She was covered in him, covered in his extraordinary love and unwavering devotion.

Creator, I thank you for this man. Of all men, you have given him to me. Let me always guard this treasure.

When she could feel the henna cracking, feel the magic sink into her skin, she pushed her lover back onto the pillows she'd set before the fire. Rising over him, she joined their bodies together, placing both hands on his shoulders as she let her head fall back in pleasure.

She let go.

Sorrow had no place here. Joy was everything. Peace was in each touch.

"I love you," she whispered. "You are the most beautiful man I have ever known." Renata opened her eyes and saw the shine in his eyes. "Don't you know that, Maxim? You brought me back to life."

He brought his hand up to cup her cheek. His finger traced her lips. "Sing to me."

Renata opened her heart and sang:

> *"Maxim of Riga, I name you*
> *My beloved. Heart's redeemer.*
> *I heard your call as I wandered*
> *In the wasteland.*
> *You found me bloody from my enemies and*
> *You spoke softly to me*
> *Calling me back to life.*
> *Beloved mate of my choosing*
> *Steward of my heart*
> *Ever faithful, always grateful*
> *I will ever be yours."*

The magic surrounded them as they made love, and when they reached their release together, Max's bright silver *talesm* shone in the darkness as Renata's gold mating marks lit and came to life.

"WE'RE ONE." She drew in the scent of smoke and magic in the air. "I didn't know what that meant until now."

"My mate." Max smiled and kissed her face, pressing his lips to her cheeks and her chin and her nose until she was giddy with love and magic and power. "My mate, Renata."

"My mate, Maxim." She could have brought a generator to life with the power of his smile.

They were lying in their bed carved with stars and flowers, enjoying the moonlight that bathed them from the window.

"Are you happy here?" he asked her.

She rested her chin on his chest. "I am happy with you. So I am happy here."

"I worried what it would be like to come back here once Thawra and Zana officially moved in. This was your home."

"But now it's not. It's a home that I love. And I love that others will grow up in the safety of these walls. I love that Zana and Thawra will make this a living place again."

"But?"

She laid her ear over his heart to hear the steady beat. "But my home is with you. Wherever we are. In a cave or in a five-star hotel. My home is with you."

Though she'd held fiercely to her independence and Max had never argued, Renata had yet to spend a night away from him since they'd come together at Midwinter. She hadn't needed to, so she hadn't wanted to. No doubt there would be times in the future where they would be forced apart. They could have assignments that sent them to opposite corners of the world.

But she would always come home to him.

Always.

He was the sword at her side, her cleft in the rock, and her surest shelter in the storm.

THE END

SONG FOR THE DYING

When a letter arrives from a remote scribe house in Latvia, Leo and Max must return to their childhood home to face the father and grandfather they've left behind. Joined by their new mates, the cousins travel north, but long-simmering tensions rise to the surface as Leo and Max explore their history and reunite with the troubled scribes who raised them.

The past is inescapable, but can it be overcome? Is it possible to build a future of happiness from a foundation of pain?

PROLOGUE

Maxim of Riga stared at the little boy across the table, narrowing his eyes and holding the measured gaze of his small opponent. Geron pursed his lips and leaned chubby elbows on the mosaic tile table, his face a study in concentration until the little boy let out an unexpected burp and burst into laughter.

Max felt Geron's laughter like birds taking flight in his chest. "I won."

"You didn't, Uncle Max!"

He stood and scooped the boy up, placing him on his shoulders. "I did. I won. You have to help me in the garden now."

"How?"

"See the apricot tree?" Max pointed to the old tree that stood at the far end of the garden at the Istanbul scribe house. The residence had been expanded the previous year when his cousin Leo had brought home a mate. "With you on my shoulders, we are going to be able to reach the very highest apricots."

"The sweet ones?"

"Yes, my friend. We will get the first apricots of the season and eat them all."

"I don't have to share with Matti?" the little boy asked about his twin sister.

"Well…" Max considered how Geron's parents would answer that, then shrugged. He wasn't a parent; he was an uncle. Entirely different thing. "Is Matti picking them?"

"No."

"Then Matti is on her own."

Their watcher, Malachi, had overseen the expansion of the property when their longtime neighbor had passed away and the family had sold the house. They had taken down the wall between the two Ottoman-style structures in the Beyoğlu neighborhood and joined the properties. The neighbor's fruit trees were only one of the benefits of the expansion.

Standing under the green leaves of the apricot tree in the first blush of summer with a wiggling, laughing child on his shoulders, Max thought about how different Geron and Matti's childhood was from his own.

Max and his cousin Leo had been raised in the Riga scribe house among warriors and grief-stricken men recovering from the chaos of the Rending. There had been no playtime or laughter in his youth. He had been trained as a soldier from the day he could pick up a sword. The only moments of respite had been when Max and Leo could escape to the woods near the house and play on their own.

Even those moments had been brief. The two boys were rarely unguarded. As two of the few surviving children of the Rending, they had been watched over obsessively. Too many others had been lost.

Matti and Geron were growing up in a new world. Not only were they part of a family, they were some of the first children of a new generation of Irin, children born to a world working toward reconciliation instead of recovering from war.

Max felt the soft brush of a rosy apricot on his cheek.

"I got one, Uncle Max."

"Good work, *myshka*." Max put the apricot in his pocket and steadied the boy on his shoulders as Geron reached for higher fruit.

Bees thrummed in the late spring sun, filling the garden with their peaceful drone. Max could hear voices in the kitchen, good-natured banter between the couples and friends who filled the house.

Since he had mated with Renata, there were three women in the scribe house. He and Renata weren't always there—they traveled in their work for the council—but Istanbul was home.

Home.

The first one Max had ever had.

LEO LIFTED his pen from the manuscript he was copying when he heard the front door open. The steps told him it was Rhys, likely returning from errands.

"Max?" Rhys called.

"In the garden," Leo said. He stretched his arms up and out, flexing shoulders that had grown stiff.

Rhys walked in the library and tossed a letter on the table. "It's addressed to both of you."

Leo picked it up cautiously, looking at the return address.

Vienna.

Soldiers rarely received personal mail. Most Irin scribes and singers had taken to the efficiency and anonymity of electronic communication with ease. Paper communication was usually reserved for watchers like Malachi or academics like Rhys.

Leo turned it over. It was addressed to Max Iverson and Leo Pēterson, the names they commonly used on human legal documents. He could feel another envelope within.

"Renata?" he called.

His new sister-in-law walked in from the kitchen. "What is it?"

"Can you call for Max, please? There's a letter addressed to both of us."

The letter was heavy in his hands. He reached for the blade he used to sharpen his quill and opened the outer envelope. He slid out the second letter—the true message—and saw the names on the front. Saw the address.

Peteris of Kurland
　　Dunte, Vidzeme
　　Watched by Riga

Leo dropped the heavy linen paper to the table, barely registering the wax seal of his father's clan or his true name on the front of the envelope. *Leontios, son of Peteris. Maxim, son of Ivo.*

Max walked in a second later and put a hand on Leo's shoulder. "What is it?"

"A letter from my father. Addressed to both of us." Leo looked up.

Max looked as confused as Leo felt. "From your *father?*"

"I haven't heard from him since I received my first assignment in Riga."

Max muttered, "Peter was never a talkative man." He nodded at the letter. "Open it."

Leo shoved it to Max. "You open it."

"Fine." Mouth set in a firm line, Max broke the wax seal on the envelope and unfolded the letter. He read for a few moments, then set the letter down in front of Leo. "I'll tell Renata and Kyra to pack."

Leo picked up the letter. It was only a few lines, which was all he would expect from the coldest, most silent man on the planet.

Leontios and Maxim,
　　Artis is dying.
　　Come home.
　　Peteris

CHAPTER ONE

Riga, Latvia

Kyra was never sure how she would be received when she visited an Irin scribe house. When she was in Istanbul, she was home. Leo was her North Star. Ava and Renata were her sisters. Max, Rhys, and Malachi the teasing, protective brothers who made life familiar. She'd been raised with her brothers, often the only woman among dozens of men. Her father, the archangel Barak, had other female children, but he kept them apart. It was part of the illusion the Fallen created to convince their daughters, the *kareshta*, that they were frightening and unstable.

It was a view shared by many of the Irin race, which was why Kyra was never sure of her reception. Renata was welcome anywhere. As one of the revered Irina singers—and a warrior no less—Renata was the hope of the future and nostalgia for the past wrapped in a confident, beautiful package.

Kyra was *other*. Traveling always made her keenly aware of that.

Max and Renata walked ahead of them in the airport, practiced travelers in almost any situation. They walked with their arms around each other, dark and light, a perfectly balanced couple.

Kyra and Leo walked behind them, following their lead as they passed through customs and immigration. Her paperwork said she was married to the man at her side. In the human world, Leo was her husband and a native Latvian. The officer looked at Kyra. Looked twice. Blinked and looked down at her paperwork one more time before his eyes went to the giant standing behind her.

She was beautiful—even those who hated her admitted that—but she was feared and distrusted by most in the Irin world. With her luminous skin and otherworldly golden eyes, she wouldn't be mistaken as human by anyone with even a drop of angelic blood. She was marked as other by humans and Irin alike.

Except for Leo.

After they passed through immigration, he slipped his hand into hers and pulled it to his mouth, kissing her knuckles before he pressed it to his chest. She could feel his heartbeat, feel the magic of his *talesm* alive on his skin. His need for her centered Kyra and refocused her attention. Being nervous was an indulgence. This trip was about Leo.

"How are you feeling?" he asked her.

"I'm fine." She squeezed his hand. "Don't be concerned about me. Are you worried?"

"About you? Always."

"No, not me. About your grandfather."

"Not worried." His deep blue eyes were fixed on some point in the distance. "I'm... sad."

"When was the last time you saw them?"

"Over one hundred years ago." His voice dropped. "Max and I didn't come back after we left the academy and received our first assignment. We had each other."

Max and Renata stood at the luggage carousel. "They didn't expect us to come back," Max said. "They had raised us and trained us. We had duties to fulfill. I'm surprised Peter even wrote us about this."

Renata passed Kyra a look that told her exactly what the other woman thought about that. Even to Kyra, whose family was the opposite of functional, it sounded heartless.

Kyra asked, "Do you know any of the men at the house here? Are any of them the same as the ones when you were young?"

Leo said, "A few."

"More than a few," Max said. "The watcher is different, but most of the soldiers are men we know."

What did that mean? Kyra sensed no anticipation or expectation of homecoming from either Max or Leo. They seemed to be on autopilot and had been since the day the letter had come.

Based on their home in Istanbul, Kyra had assumed Irin families were stronger than the fractured bonds between children of the Fallen. Perhaps she'd been wrong. Perhaps nothing would be what she expected. She gripped Leo's hand more tightly.

Whatever came, Leo was hers and she was his. Of that she had no doubt.

RENATA WAS TRYING her best not to let the anger she was feeling bleed into Max. They were mated, and Max was unusually perceptive of her moods, often identifying what she was feeling before she did. It was part of the reason they worked so well together. But for this trip he needed support, comfort, and strength, not anger.

She wasn't angry at *him* of course. She was angry *for* him. She'd known his childhood hadn't been a happy one. Unlike Renata, Max and Leo had grown up after the Rending. They had no memories of a balanced home with Irina influence. They had been little more than valuable child soldiers to the Riga scribes. Max had once casually mentioned sword training at the age of six.

Renata's head had almost exploded.

They walked outside and waited for a minivan to taxi them to an address on the other side of the city. Max loaded their luggage in the back of the van, then slid next to Renata, reaching his arm behind her to pull her close.

"Okay?" she asked.

Max only nodded.

Renata's childhood in the mountains of northern Italy had been one of stories and adventure and indulgence. As the only daughter of two librarians, she'd been surrounded by Irin history and lore. Imagination and creativity had been cultivated. From speaking with Rhys and Malachi, she knew they'd had similar childhoods. Protected and indulged in Irin communities until it was time to start training at thirteen.

Max and Leo had started at six. Possibly earlier. They had been raised to be soldiers by hardened men. The only family they had had cast them into war as soon as they'd reached maturity.

If Renata bit her tongue any harder, the tip would fall off.

It was after rush hour, but the days were long in Latvian summers. Cars zipped by them as their silent taxi headed northeast from the airport to the Mežaparks neighborhood.

It was Renata's first visit to Riga. Max didn't keep a home here. She'd never heard him mention going back, though he'd had an apartment in Oslo as long as she'd known him. As far as Renata had been able to tell, Riga was a quiet and safe city, so Max would have little reason to visit.

Mežaparks was a thickly wooded neighborhood of large homes and gated estates seven kilometers north of the city center. The sky was still a pale grey-blue when they pulled up to the old house and parked by the gate. Renata could hear dogs barking in the distance, but no one waited for them.

Leo buzzed the keypad on the gate as the taxi pulled away.

"Did you call anyone?" Leo asked.

"No. They'll be expecting us. They're the ones who sent the letter from Peter."

It was telling to Renata that Leo did not call his father by any title. Max didn't call him uncle. He was Peter. Their grandfather was Artis.

Leo shoved his hands in his pockets. "Maybe we should have called."

"I told you—"

The speaker on the keypad crackled. "Yes?"

Renata looked around the entry, but she could see no cameras or modern surveillance equipment.

Max bent down. "Tell the watcher Maxim and Leontios have arrived from Istanbul."

"Along with our mates," Leo added.

"A moment."

A buzzing sound signaled their welcome. Renata pushed the gate open, reaching for the bag she'd hastily packed.

"We were expecting you, brothers." A different crackling voice. "We did not know you were bringing your mates. They are most welcome."

The speaker went silent, and Renata held the gate as Max, Leo, and Kyra grabbed their luggage. Leo, as usual, was treating Kyra as if she were made of glass. Renata tried not to roll her eyes. Her sister-in-law was a capable woman with a strong mind. She'd fooled Renata on first meeting but had quickly revealed an iron will and an excellent understanding of human nature. Renata approved of her new sister wholeheartedly. The two women were as different as night and day, but then so were Leo and Max.

Leo cosseted his mate, but Renata couldn't find fault. They were too happy. Too adoring of each other. Kyra had lived most of her life with a wolf at her back. If it gave Leo pleasure to pamper her, Renata would never criticize.

Max grunted beside her as he threw a second backpack filled with books over his shoulder. "What did you pack in here? Is this my bag or yours? I don't remember packing anything this heavy. Why aren't you carrying this?"

Ah, her doting lover. "I packed your travel desk and the

manuscript you were working on in Italy. You haven't had time to work on it since we got back to Istanbul."

"You think I'll have time here?"

She slipped her hand into his. "We are here until he is gone, aren't we? In times of waiting, it is good to have things to do." Renata could feel Max's eyes on her. "What?"

"I love you."

The warm weight of his words settled in her chest. "I know."

They walked up the driveway through an alley of linden trees, taller oaks dotting the property. The house was set back from the road, three stories tall with golden windows shining in the dusk. The front door opened and two figures appeared in silhouette.

"Is that Volos?" Leo asked.

"I think so."

"He cut his hair."

Renata said, "Well, it has been roughly one hundred years. He might have wanted a new look."

Both Leo and Max looked at her as if she were speaking a foreign language. Only Kyra offered her the ghost of a smile.

"He is coming," Kyra said.

The scribe that approached didn't say a word. He appeared middle-aged, and his face was lined. His hair was a rough crop of grey and brown, and he wore a trimmed beard. He paused a few feet before he reached them and stared, first at Renata and Kyra, then at Max and Leo.

"Volos," Max said. "It is good to see you well."

Volos nodded to them, then he bent down and reached for Renata's suitcase. He hoisted it over his shoulder, then reached for Max's bag. "I'll get the others if you want to leave them here," he muttered.

"It's fine," Leo said. "Thank you, brother."

Volos nodded and turned back to the house. Max took one of the bags from Leo's shoulder and kept walking.

"He's a talkative one," Renata said.

"Just you wait," Max said. "Compared to the rest of them, Volos is a comedian."

———

KYRA STUDIED her plate as she ate, resting a hand on Leo's leg under the table. Her mate was uncanny at understanding when she was uncomfortable, and Kyra had been uncomfortable the moment she walked through the door.

None of the scribes had said anything rude. None of the scribes had said anything at all. But they watched. She could feel their eyes examining. As Max and Renata engaged the new watcher of the house—a friendly Dutch scribe named Levi—Kyra and Leo ate on the other side of the table. The meal was simple, a bowl of lamb stew, bread, and fresh milk. It smelled delicious, but Kyra barely tasted it. Five other scribes joined them at the dining table.

Volos, the scribe who had carried in their luggage. A tall Russian called Kaz, who looked like he could be related to Max and Leo. Two men who hadn't said a word, not even to introduce themselves, and a thin man who stared openly at Kyra. All of them were European except for one of the silent men. He had massive shoulders and long, dark hair tied back in a braid. Kyra guessed he was Northern or Central Asian. She wondered how he had arrived in this cold and silent city on the edge of the Baltic Sea.

"Fricis," Leo said to the thin man, who was staring at Kyra. "How have you been? How is the library?"

"Fine." He didn't stop staring.

Leo radiated tension. "Did you have a question?"

The man asked something in a language Kyra didn't understand.

"English," Max said sharply from the other end of the table. "Not everyone here speaks Russian."

"Does she sing?" the man asked in a precise accent.

"Who?" Renata asked. "Me? Of course I sing. Haven't you met an

Irina before? Max said all of you were older than him and Leo. I would have thought you'd met Irina before."

Fricis cut his eyes to Renata, clearly annoyed. "I'm not—"

"I am learning," Kyra said quietly. She appreciated her new sister trying to divert attention away from the foreign object in the room, but the questions wouldn't go away until they were answered. "I know some magic, but I'm still learning. Most of what I've learned so far has been for self-defense."

The large man across from Leo grunted. "Good sense." He glanced up from his bowl of stew and met Kyra's eyes. "I am Gustav. I am the weapons master here. If you or your mate need daggers, I can provide them."

Kyra's eyes went wide. "Thank you."

"We appreciate that, Gustav." Leo squeezed her hand. "Kyra is quite good with daggers. Her brother has given her lessons, and she's also trained with Renata."

"But you're teaching her magic?" Fricis directed the question at Renata. "Irina magic?"

"Of course I am," Renata said, her voice icy. "She's my sister. Why wouldn't I?"

The man opened his mouth again, but Levi interrupted. "Fricis is our archivist and naturally curious," he said. "I hope you're not offended by his questions. It has been many years since any Irina have visited us."

Renata said, "Perhaps after we are finished eating our meal, I can sing for you. I know a beautiful version of 'Adelina and the Giant.' That is a popular local song in this area, is it not?"

The scribes around the table murmured agreement, and Kyra noticed the atmosphere in the room warmed.

Levi said, "You honor us, sister." He turned to Kyra. "We would love to hear from Kyra too. If she would like to join you."

Kyra could feel the heat in her face. "I am still learning. But thank you."

"Your next visit." Gustav nodded as if the matter was settled. "You can sing for us then."

Kyra didn't know if Leo and Max would have any desire to visit Riga in the future, but she nodded anyway. Better to be polite and discuss the matter with Leo in private. The weapons master and the watcher were welcoming. The other men were harder to read. They were cold and hard, like frozen earth that hadn't seen the sun in years.

After their simple meal, they moved to the great room while Volos and Kaz cleared the dishes. The house in Riga was a beautiful old mansion with carved wood paneling and spacious rooms, but the furnishings were spare. If Kyra didn't know better, she'd have thought the men of the house had just moved in. Furniture was heavy and simple. There was no art or decoration. The only things that passed for adornment were the rows of immaculate weapons and old armor mounted on the walls of the great room where a large fireplace burned.

Kyra and Leo sat on a large sofa in the back of the room as Renata took a place by the central fireplace. Her tall figure dominated the space as the scribes gathered around her to listen. Kyra could feel the expectation in the air.

"How long has it been?" Kyra asked Leo quietly.

"What?"

"How long since these men have heard an Irina sing?"

Leo's face went blank. "I don't know. I never heard any Irina song in these halls."

"Hundreds of years?" Kyra asked. "Since before the Rending?"

Leo only shrugged.

She had listened to Renata sing many times in Istanbul. Her sister was a trained Irina librarian and could recite oral histories for days if asked. It was part of her training to share her knowledge, and she'd taken on the job of teaching Kyra and Ava with pleasure. Max sat beside her on the stone hearth, his hand resting on the back of Renata's thigh as she stood before the scribes.

Kyra remembered the first time she'd seen Max. It had been years before Kostas had revealed her as his sister, and she'd seen the dangerous Irin scribe from the corner of a café in Sofia where Max met with her brother. His gaze had been dark and suspicious then, his energy restless and savage. Kyra had escaped through the back door of the café with one of her brother's men, worried Max might look in her direction.

Now his eyes rested on his mate, peace and pride in his gaze. The darkness was still visible when Max was roused, but Kyra could see past it to the protective bent of his nature. He and Renata were perfectly matched—warriors who'd found respite in each other.

Kyra leaned over to Leo. "They're so beautiful together."

Leo's face softened. "As beautiful as we are?"

She smiled. "Maybe more."

"Not possible." He kissed her temple, and Kyra laid her head on his shoulder as Renata began to sing. She sang in the Old Language, which Kyra was still learning, so Leo whispered the translation in her ear.

> "Listen this night to the song of Adelina's journey,
> our sister who sailed to the northern sea.
> She met many along the water and battled many demons,
> but none matched her wit, save for the giant of Saaremaa."

It was a story like many Kyra had heard in other traditions and languages. An adventurer traveling far from home, outsmarting enemies and fighting foes. Adelina traveled from an unnamed land in the east and followed the rivers to the Baltic Sea where she met a giant who promised to give her secret knowledge from the Forgiven angels if she could outwit him. After many days, Adelina discovered the answer to his riddle hidden in a linden tree and told the giant, who told her the secret of his long and happy marriage. Of course, the secret knowledge the giant shared involved building

SONG FOR THE DYING

saunas and growing cabbage, which made everyone in the room laugh even though they'd all heard the tale before.

It was a joyful and humorous story, one meant to be shared among friends after a full meal. The low chuckles and smiles around the room accomplished what Renata had likely wanted. The heavy atmosphere lifted, and the hard men began to smile.

Renata moved from Adelina's journey to a joyful song about the first mothers, the venerated women who had raised the first generation of Irin children. It was a song Kyra had heard before, a common and popular one glowing with praise and beautiful imagery. She glanced around the room to see the softer faces of the scribes around her. Some of them wore wistful expressions. Gustav had glassy eyes.

"They needed this," Kyra whispered. "They needed her."

Leo nodded but didn't speak.

When Renata moved into the next song, Kyra felt the energy in the room change. The air grew heavy, and she could feel magic rising. "Leo?" She tugged on his arm. "What is she singing?"

Leo's own eyes were glassy, and his voice was rough. "It's a mourning song. 'Hilal's Lament.'"

Renata kept singing even as tears began to fill her eyes. Max leaned into her, his arm wrapped around his mate's legs as she poured two hundred years of mourning into her voice. Mating marks lit around her neck, gold that matched the fire behind her. Max's *talesm* glowed in response.

"Please," Kyra whispered. "Tell me what she's saying."

Leo gripped her hand. He whispered,

> "Surely I will sing of my lover's hands,
> strong in battle and gentle in the night.
> He has left me, but I will not fade.
> For our children cry from the meadow
> where their father fell.
> They eat the bloody earth in mourning

and rage at the night."

Kyra watched the hard-faced warriors around them. No eye was dry. They wiped their tears without shame, listening to the singer's lament. Some bent over themselves as if in physical pain. Their *talesm* glowed with a low silver light, and Kyra saw nearly all of them wore mourning collars around their neck, visible when their magic was roused. The silent Asian scribe on the far side of the room wore a thick mourning collar for his mate with three finer circles beneath it symbolizing the loss of three children, likely dead in the Rending.

Kyra's heart ached for them, these hard men who were so very alone. No children laughed in their halls. No joyful songs filled their house. They trudged on, half-alive, ensuring the balance of light and dark in the world with no hope of a brighter future or the comfort of their ancestors.

They simply endured.

> *"So I must guide my children back to light*
> *that their hearts do not turn to stone.*
> *They will be my birds in the nest*
> *like larks in the morning,*
> *singing to bring the sun's return."*

CHAPTER TWO

They packed a borrowed Land Cruiser for Dunte the next morning. Leo and Volos were loading the bags. Gustav had given them several weapons he needed Peter to repair at his forge. Max and Renata were having a heated discussion under the trees. Kyra was sleeping in the back seat.

The sun had warmed the leather bench of the Land Cruiser, and she'd drifted to sleep before Leo came downstairs with the first pieces of luggage. She hadn't rested much the night before. Leo had taken her to bed, holding her silently while she lay sleepless. When emotions were high, as they had been during Renata's singing, it was nearly impossible for her to shut out the voices around her.

It wasn't that her defenses were thin. She had extraordinary perception, even for an Irina. It was why he'd been willing to translate for her the night before. She would have perceived the sorrow in the room. Better for her to understand what had provoked it.

Volos glanced at Kyra. "She's delicate."

Leo tried not to bristle. "She's stronger than she looks."

Volos shrugged. "I didn't say she wasn't strong. My Naina was delicate. A spider's silk is delicate; that doesn't mean it's not strong."

Leo carefully packed the swords behind the suitcases. "I've never heard you talk about your mate."

Volos grunted. "You were a boy."

"Not when I came back from the academy, I wasn't."

Volos frowned. "You didn't understand then. You couldn't have." *You didn't have a mate.*

Leo couldn't argue with the older scribe. Loving Kyra had taught him both bravery and weakness. Even the thought of losing her paralyzed him. He couldn't even bring himself to imagine it; the places it took him in his mind were too dark.

"How did you survive?" Leo asked without thinking.

Volos's face was hard. "You don't have a choice."

"Others chose—"

"I cannot face my Naina in the heavens," Volos said, "if I haven't fulfilled my duty on the earth."

The rate of suicide in the weeks and months after the Rending had been high. They didn't call it suicide, of course. But countless scribes died in reckless battles. Others performed magic that could only poison them in the end. Many who had lost their mates and children simply slept and did not wake.

For the first time, Leo realized that the cold men who'd raised him had been faced with a choice, and despite their many faults, they'd chosen to stay alive. Looking at Kyra sleeping in the back of the car, Leo finally understood how difficult that choice must have been. The scribes who raised him might not have been warm or affectionate men, but they had remained.

Leo held out his hand. "Thank you for teaching me how to ride a horse when I was ten. My father should have done it, but he never did. When you found out, you made me work with you in the stables every morning. You taught me without telling anyone because you knew I was embarrassed."

Volos took Leo's hand. "Your father had a duty too. That was all he had after Lauma died."

No, he still had a son.

"He's not patrolling anymore?" Leo asked. "Levi said Peter was only forging weapons. He takes commissions from all over the world now, huh?"

Volos shrugged. "He's taking care of Artis, and Artis won't leave Dunte. Taking care of Artis is his only duty now. The forge just keeps him out of trouble."

Taking care of Artis was his father's duty.

But Artis was dying.

So what did a scribe do without duty when duty was his only reason to live?

———

"IT WASN'T NECESSARY." Max's arms were crossed over his chest.

"I don't agree. It was completely necessary." Renata spoke in a measured voice. "It may have made you uncomfortable, and I'm sure it made them uncomfortable. But helping our people to grieve is why those songs exist. Singing them brings healing along with the pain."

"Did you know Ganbaatar had three children?"

"I don't know who Gan—"

"The Mongolian scribe. Did you know they were all slaughtered? His mate drowned herself because she failed to protect their children." Max didn't know why he was so angry. "You think singing about a lark in the morning is going to heal a wound like that?"

Renata's mouth was set in a stubborn line. "Have you forgotten I am well-acquainted with grief? It's my duty to help them, whether it pleases me or not."

A wave of guilt shut his mouth. It was only a few months before that a small child had given Renata an outlet to vent her own grief. And that small child had suffered as a result. It had cost that child to comfort Renata. "It hurt you," he said. "To sing that lament hurt you."

"Of course it did." Her expression softened. "But it's part of the reason I exist. If Midwinter taught me anything, it's that I'm more than a soldier. I'm still a keeper of memories, Max. It's what I'm meant to do."

He hooked an arm around her neck and pulled her close. "This place, Reni..."

"I know." She slid her arms around his waist. "I know."

They stood in the shadow of the oaks and lindens, morning dew wetting their feet from the uncut grass that grew like a wild meadow. Max wanted to take his shoes off and run under the trees like the feral child he'd once been. He wanted to run away.

"Singing a lament isn't going to heal all their wounds. And maybe nothing will ever heal them completely. But it's a step in the journey, Max. Just like this journey you and Leo have to take. You don't have to know the whole path. You can't. Right now you just have to take the next step."

Max's anger lifted with Renata's gentle words, and the true reason he'd snapped at his mate became clear. "I don't want to go to Dunte."

"I know. But you will. And you're going to face your uncle and your grandfather. You're going to be with your cousin when he speaks to his father."

"Peter is a bastard," Max said. "He doesn't deserve a son like Leo. At least my father had the decency to die an honorable death. Peter just lingered in the back of Leo's life, resenting his own son for keeping him alive."

Renata put both her hands on Max's cheeks. "Leo is going to try to take care of everyone because that's who he is. We have to take care of him."

Max nodded. He could take care of Leo. He'd been doing it since they were children. Someone had to live in the dark corners so Leo could remain the lark singing in the morning. Because Renata was right—their world desperately needed that bright song, and if there was a pure Irin soul in existence, it was his cousin.

MAX AND LEO sat in the front as they drove the fifty-five kilometers north to the village on the edge of the Gulf of Riga. Kyra slept in the back while Renata worked on her tablet and occasionally took pictures out the window. The journey was silent as Leo watched the streets of the city give way to the patched pavement of the countryside north of the capital. The road ran in a quiet curve, north through wooded villages and farmland that edged toward the sea.

"Do you remember going on horseback?" Leo asked.

"Yes." Max was behind the wheel. "It took longer."

"It was a nice trip though. I think riding horses along the coast was one of the few times Artis was ever happy."

"Music," Max said. "He was happy when he was playing the guitar."

"I don't know about happy. He was content."

"Yes." Max eased the car into a curve in the road. "*Content* is a better word."

Leo cracked open the window to smell the country air. It was night-and-day different from the dusty and spice-laden air of Istanbul. Latvia smelled of green woods and hay and the sea. "Did you call Malachi this morning?"

"I did. Nothing out of the ordinary at home. He says we can take as much time as we need."

Leo was unsettled by the idea of an indefinite stay in Dunte. The farm they were going to had been his mother and aunt's childhood home. There had once been a small community of Irin in the nearby village, which was known for excellent ceramics and ironwork. Their grandfather had been a respected sword maker and blacksmith.

There had been a farm with a large cowshed and many outbuildings, one of them an ancient forge. They grew vegetables. They tended apples. There was a great outdoor oven that his grandfather maintained with care, though it was barely used. Perhaps his grandmother had been a baker. Leo and Max had no idea.

They had no idea about any of their dead family. The dead were not spoken of. They didn't know how or where their mothers had been trained. They had no idea how Lauma had met Peteris or Stasya had met Ivo. Leo knew his father was not from Latvia, but he didn't know where he was born or who his people were. And Max's father was a complete mystery; all they knew was his name.

Memories of the dead inhabited the farm like ghosts dancing in the corner of a vision. Leo had once found a pony carved into an old apple tree in the orchard. Max saw scribbles low on the wall of a closet. A forgotten note fell from the seam of a book.

The Irin village was long gone, but the ghosts of their mothers lingered in Dunte. Leo hoped they lingered because his mother and aunt had been happy. That was his hope. Whether he had any reason for it was debatable.

"Almost there," Max murmured. "You might want to wake your woman."

Leo reached back and rubbed Kyra's knee as Max pulled off the main road and onto a track leading into a dense copse of trees. It was only wide enough for one vehicle and overgrown by weeds and spruce branches. As they bumped over the dirt road, he felt Kyra stretch and move.

"Are we there?" she asked in a sleepy voice.

"Almost." Renata tucked her tablet in a backpack and leaned forward, placing her hand on Max's shoulder. "So, is there plumbing in this place?"

"There's a well on the property," Max said. "Gustav said Peter has modernized it over the years. He did most of the work himself, but he's very good with most machines, so there will likely be plumbing of some kind."

"As long as there's water, I can manage," Renata said. All of them had been born before plumbing was common. She took a deep breath and smiled. "I smell the sea! And cows."

"We're close to both," Leo said. "The Gulf of Riga is just past those trees. You can walk to the shore from the farm."

"That's so nice," Kyra murmured. "I love the sea. I miss the beaches in Bulgaria."

"It's not warm," Max said. "Not even in the summer. You've been warned."

"That's okay." Kyra reached for Leo's hand. "I can still walk on the shore."

"And ride," Leo said. "If Peter still has horses."

They rounded a curve of the dirt track, and the farm came into view. Leo had thought he was prepared to see it again.

He wasn't.

A large farmhouse with a straw-thatched roof dominated the yard. Across the mud-and-grass yard was a tall barn with a pen on one side. A horse was hobbled in the pasture, grazing on green grass while three cows meandered through an orchard in the distance, their bells tolling through the midmorning air.

Leo rolled down his window and was greeted with the familiar smell that took him directly back to his childhood. Sea air. Straw. A hint of manure.

"What a beautiful barn," Renata said. "It must have been a sizable dairy at one point."

"I think it was," Max said. "But not when we were children. We only kept a few cows for milk and cheese. We didn't sell anything."

"Did you live here or in Riga?" Kyra asked.

"Both places," Leo said. "Artis was always here. We spent the week in Riga with Peter, training at the scribe house. Then weekends and most of the summer here with Peter and Artis, learning how to forge."

"And milk cows," Max muttered. "And plant cabbage. And dig weeds."

"You know how to forge?" Renata squeezed Max's shoulder. "I didn't know that."

"I haven't done it in over a hundred years," he said. "Leo kept it up longer than I did."

Because Max couldn't wait to escape anything having to do with Peter. Leo glanced at Max and saw his stony face. "It's a useful skill, even if you're assigned to a house with a good smith."

Leo saw someone walk out of the farmhouse door and stand on the wooden steps. The giant man had dark hair and light skin. Leo thought he could see Peter's unusual green eyes from this distance, but it was probably only a memory. His father's eyes weren't blue like Leo and Max's. They were green like seaweed bleached in the sand. He and Max had both gotten their coloring from their mothers, but they came from tall people on both sides. Peter was well over six feet tall and broad as the side of their barn, his chest and arms bulky from smithing. Artis was just as tall, slightly thinner, with a body similarly hardened by the forge.

Max parked the car, but none of them opened the doors.

Leo glanced at his cousin, who was staring at Peter with narrowed eyes. Leo reached for Max's hand on the gearshift, squeezed it, and said, "It's fine. Come. It will be fine."

Max turned to Leo. "I won't hold my tongue. I'm not a boy anymore."

"I wouldn't ask you to."

Max gave Leo a slight nod; then he released his grip on the shift and opened the door. He got out and opened Renata's door for her, grabbing her hand before he walked to meet Peter.

Leo opened his door and got out. Kyra's door was already open, but he held it for her as she climbed out and stretched, avoiding the mud in the farmyard. He put a hand on her cheek and bent down to take her lips.

That simple touch gave him life. Kyra slid her hand along the back of Leo's neck and pressed herself closer. Her touch told him without words: *I adore you. You are mine.* Leo released her lips and rested his forehead against hers.

"Thank you for loving me," he whispered.

She kissed the corner of his mouth. "Introduce me to your father, Leo. Remember, he cannot be worse than mine."

Leo's smile was immediate and bright. "I suppose you're right."

"That's the one benefit of mating with a *kareshta*." She slid her hand in his and pushed his shoulder to turn him around. "You'll win the less-evil-family contest every single time."

———

HAND IN RENATA'S, Max approached his uncle. The man looked exactly as he had the last time Max had seen him. He hadn't aged at all—he was keeping up his longevity spells—though grey touched the wild hair he tied back with a leather strap.

They did not embrace. That wasn't something they did in their family. But Peter stared at Renata with a look Max couldn't decipher, and it wasn't unwelcoming.

"Does the fire still burn in this house?" Max asked, the formal greeting of the Irin giving him the script he needed in the moment.

"It does," Peter answered. "And you are welcome to its light." He glanced at Renata, then past them to Leo and Kyra. "You and your own."

Max inclined his head but didn't release Renata. "Uncle, this is my mate, Renata von Meren, a singer of the Istanbul house."

"Well met in this place, Renata." Peter inclined his head. "You honor us with your voice."

"Welcomed with grace," Renata said. "I'm happy to be here."

"I am Peteris of Dunte, son of Artis." He paused, his eyes drawn to Leo even as he tried to address Renata. "I am Maxim's uncle."

"I know," Renata said. "And Leo's father."

Leo and Kyra stopped in the middle of the yard. "Peter," Leo said, gripping Kyra's hand. "This is my mate, Kyra."

That indefinable look flickered in Peter's eyes again.

"Well met, Leontios." Peter's voice cracked. "And Kyra." He tore his eyes from them and looked at the barn. "I need... the cows. The cows need to be milked." He motioned toward the house. "You know your home. Artis is in the library."

Max heard the bells coming closer as the cows heard their master's voice and walked back from the orchard with full udders. It was midmorning, and the fact that they hadn't already been milked surprised Max. It also told him that Peter was distracted.

Renata stepped forward to greet the cows. "I'll help you. I like cows."

Peter nodded. "Very well."

Kyra released Leo's hand and walked through the kitchen garden, past the porch to the massive outdoor oven between the farmhouse and the orchard. She walked around it, her hand running over the whitewashed walls. Peter paused and watched her.

"This is beautiful," she said, her entrancing voice capturing everyone's attention. "Does it still work?"

Kyra didn't speak much, but when she did, it was impossible to ignore her. Max couldn't explain it other than to say his sister's voice was magnetic. She was a first-generation daughter of an archangel; everything about her was magnetic. But there was something special about her voice. No one was immune. Not even Peter, who walked toward her.

"It was Evelina's," Peter said. "Artis's mate. It still works, but we do not bake. We buy our bread from a woman in the village."

Kyra's smile was open and bright. "If I could get some wood for it, I can bake. I had an oven similar to this in Bulgaria. It was very relaxing, and Artis might enjoy fresh bread."

All Peter could do was nod. He looked as if he wanted to say more, but he stopped, turned, and walked to the barn with Renata behind him.

Leo came to Max's side. "We should have brought women home years ago."

"It wouldn't have worked," Max said.

"Don't you think so?" He nodded at Peter. "Look at him. He's actually speaking."

"It wouldn't have worked because we needed to bring these women." He watched his warrior mate guide the milk cows into the barn, patting them on their backs and trying to engage Peter in conversation. "Only them."

CHAPTER THREE

I f Kyra had tried imagining Leo's grandfather, she would have imagined an older, white-haired, bushy-bearded version of her mate. And her imagination would have been very close to reality. Artis of Dunte, elder scribe and master smith, sat in a round chair facing the sun. He was a tall man, his long legs stretched out in front of him. He was a little stooped by age and displayed no apparent signs of sickness.

But Kyra could see what the others could not. Artis was not sick; he was tired.

She had seen the same look on countless Grigori and *kareshta* faces in her life. Unlike the Irin, who could harness magic to prolong their lives infinitely, children of the Fallen all died eventually. They lived longer than humans, but with no Forgiven magic to prolong their life, they were mortal. They persisted in perfect health, untouched by old age, until one day they simply ran out, like a toy whose workings had broken from too much use. Sometimes they lingered in a coma for a few days or their heart would give out suddenly. Then they would return to the heavens, a swirl of dust rising in the air.

If Leo had not mated with Kyra, sharing his magic with her, it would have been her own fate as well.

Artis opened his eyes and turned his face from the sun as Kyra entered the library with a tray of warm bread spread with butter and mugs of fresh milk. The corner of his mouth turned up. It reminded Kyra of Max.

He said, "The food of the angels."

"Bread?"

"Bread." He rose and walked to the table. "Fresh bread and milk."

"Turkish people consider bread sacred, but they eat so much meat." Kyra set the tray on the table. "I'm not accustomed to it. I prefer bread."

"Turks are a herding people," Artis said, sitting down in the smooth wooden chair. "Herding people eat meat. We are farming and fishing people here. We eat fish and what we can grow."

"And milk." Kyra sat across from him and raised her mug.

Artis lifted his mug to her. "And milk. The best milk in the world."

It *was* delicious milk. She'd visited the market in town their first afternoon at the farm to gather supplies. Eggs, milk, and all the vegetables they could eat could be found at the farm, but they needed flour to bake bread. Oil to cook. A bit of meat, though Leo and Max—normally heavy meat eaters—were happy to eat the egg-and-vegetable frittata Renata had baked the night before supplemented by the smoked fish Peter had caught.

"This place reminds me of a farm we stayed at in Germany. There were apples in the cellar and cabbage in the garden." Kyra had explored everything, including the path that led from the woods and meadows down to the ocean. "I was young then. My father had a compound there."

"Barak?" Artis's lip no longer curled at the name. "Did you stay there with your brother?"

"Yes."

"The Grigori?"

"Yes, my brothers are all Grigori," Kyra repeated. "Free Grigori."

Artis grunted and bit into his bread. The night before when Leo had told his grandfather Kyra's parentage, the reaction had been involuntary and instant. It hadn't surprised Kyra, though Leo and Max had been offended. Barak was one of the Fallen, a sworn enemy of the Irin scribes, and she was his daughter. Even if her sire had redeemed himself in his death, Artis had lived for hundreds of years seeing Barak's children as deadly enemies.

"We get news," he said. "We do get news up here. That young watcher in Riga forces it on us. Visits once a month whether we want him or not. So I know what you are."

Kyra leaned her elbow on the table. "I know what you are too."

"A stubborn, narrow-minded old man?"

"My mate's grandfather," she said. "And... the monster in the night."

Artis sat up straight. "We weren't the monsters."

Kyra shrugged. "My sisters and I didn't know that. The only ones who protected us were our brothers. Sometimes they went out at night and didn't come back because of the scribes. I didn't know why. I only knew they were gone and it was because of the tattooed men."

"Hmm." Clearly Artis hadn't thought of life from Grigori perspective. He peered at her from beneath bushy eyebrows. "Do his *talesm* frighten you?"

"Leo's?" Kyra was surprised. Artis was the first scribe to ever ask her that. Even Leo hadn't thought of it. "At first they frightened me very much. All of them did. But not anymore. I love Leo, and his *talesm* are part of who he is."

"As it should be."

His gruff response belied the thoughtful look in his blue eyes. They were the same blue as Leo and Max's. Vivid sky blue that always made Kyra feel as if she were sitting in sunshine when Leo looked at her.

"Leo and Max have your eyes."

"Both my grandsons look very much like me." Artis set down his milk. "Leo is broader like his father, and Max is thinner like his."

Kyra thought of all the questions she and Renata had discussed between them when Leo and Max weren't around. "Who was Max's father? We know his name but not who he was."

"He was a troublemaker!" Artis coughed out a laugh. "And wasn't he the perfect match for my Stasya? I always wanted her to find a steady one like Lauma found with Peteris. Thought it might calm her down. But Ivo's father ordered a sword from me and Ivo came to fetch it." Artis's hand slammed down on the table, making Kyra jump. "And that was that. *Reshon.* I could see it in the both of them the first time they met. Stasya and Ivo were both wild things. Wild for each other. Wild for life."

Artis closed his eyes at the memory, and Kyra watched his face droop. The man who could be so vital when he spoke looked frail and ephemeral in silence.

"How long have you been fading?" Kyra asked.

Artis opened his eyes. "I stopped my longevity spells the day Leo and Max left for the academy."

"A hundred years?"

He cleared his throat. "More."

Once he had stopped his longevity spells, Artis had begun to fade just as Kyra's Grigori brothers did. It made sense. Artis was old, but he still appeared in near-perfect health. His soul was aging, not his body. The truth was in his eyes.

Kyra decided to change the subject. "What about Leo? Were his parents *reshon* too?"

Artis shook his head. "I don't know. They didn't speak of it if they were. Peteris was so quiet. He was sent from Riga to apprentice with me. Did he tell you that?"

"No," Kyra said. "He doesn't speak much."

"He doesn't speak at all." Renata walked in from the kitchen with her own plate. "Unless he's talking about the farm or swords. Kyra, this bread is delicious."

"Thank you for making the butter."

"Eh." Renata sat down. "I made Max do it. He was out of practice."

The old man cackled.

"Don't tell me you know how to churn butter, old man," Renata said. "You were probably just like my father. Pathetic at household chores."

"And you're like my Stasya," Artis reached over and pinched the air in front of her. "Bite, bite, bite. But I know how to make butter. I know how to do everything to keep young boys fed."

Of course he did. There hadn't been anyone else.

"Keep telling stories," Renata said. "Heaven knows Max and Leo haven't told us anything."

From what Kyra could tell, Max and Leo didn't know. They didn't speak about the past in this family, but age and impending death had loosened Artis's tongue.

He said, "I don't think I heard Lauma and Peter say a dozen words to each other in the year he was working with me." Artis let out a weak cough. "But then Lauma marches in here—this very room—and says, '*Tēti!* Peteris and I will be mated in two weeks. Be sure to send the letter to his family.' And that was that." He shrugged massive shoulders. "Peter was the same solemn scribe he'd ever been, but he smiled at Lauma and Lauma adored him." He nodded at Kyra. "She looked at him the way you look at Leo. So yes, maybe they were *reshon*. How to make sense of it otherwise?"

"You had two daughters," Renata said. "No other children?"

Artis's eyes lost focus. "How could we have asked for more? With blessings like those two? We tempted fate, I think."

"Why?" Renata asked. "Because they died? Many died. My whole family died. You had two grandsons remaining. And a son-in-law. You were luckier than most."

Artis raised his eyebrows. "You have a sharp tongue."

"And?"

"Keep a whetstone handy. You'll need a sharp tongue with Maxim."

Renata laughed, and Kyra couldn't hide her smile. Renata reached for Artis's empty plate. "I'll get you more." She rose and left the room.

"I'm not hungry," he said. "But I do enjoy being fussed over."

"Shall I get you more milk?" Kyra rose, but Artis grabbed her wrist. It startled Kyra, and she felt a jolt of energy move from her skin to his. "Artis?"

He released her immediately. "So much power," he said, flexing his hand. "Do you burn him when he touches you, daughter of the Fallen?"

Kyra bit back her first response. He was an old man, set in his ways. "I would never hurt Leo. He is the other part of me."

Artis raised his eyes. "You have gold eyes like my Evelina. Even brighter than hers."

"She had Leoc's blood?" Ava had told her only those with Leoc's blood retained the amber gold color of angelic eyes.

Artis's eyes narrowed. "She had a touch."

It was more than a touch. Kyra said, "You said she was a baker."

"She was a baker because she wanted to be a baker. But she saw things too. Her parents didn't want her leaving the village, so they didn't force her into seer training."

"But is that why she was killed? Because she was a seer?"

Artis drew back. "They were all killed. Not for any reason. Simply to break us, I think."

She could see him drawing into himself. He turned his face back into the sun that filled the corner of the room and closed his eyes. She felt the weight of his grief like an old wound. It no longer bled, it ached, begging to be relieved.

A week. If that. Kyra had seen those weary eyes before.

Artis would be gone within a week.

Renata couldn't find Max in the house, so she went out to the woods and followed the trail that led down to the sea. She stepped on the worn path, letting the breeze surround her, and followed it down a small hill toward the sound of water and seagulls.

When the sun touched her skin, she could feel the summer warmth, but more often she walked in the crisp cool of the pines. She hadn't found any occupied houses for miles. There seemed to be a few vacation homes along this stretch of the coast, but they were all empty.

Forest gave way to rolling dunes covered in grass and low green shrubs. Max sat on a rise of sand, his hands braced behind him, staring at the tide washing out. The ocean was grey that afternoon. In the distance, the deeper blue of the water gave way to a bright, cloud-spotted sky.

She walked behind her mate and sat down, stretching her legs on either side and wrapping her arms around his back. Max leaned into her, loosely holding her hands over his heart.

Renata leaned down and whispered, "Did all the butter-churning wear you out? I promise I'll be more gentle next time."

Max's chest rumbled with a laugh. "Woman..." He sighed. "You give me peace."

"I love you." It still thrilled her every time she said it. She pressed her cheek to his temple and let him lean on her, borrowing her strength.

They'd made love silently the night before. Quiet tenderness as she wrapped her arm around his shoulders and pressed her lips to his neck. They had eased each other into release, falling asleep with arms and legs entwined, holding on to each other even as they slept.

Max was so brash. So confident. But not in Dunte. Not in the shadow of his uncle and grandfather, who lived with the ghosts of their people.

"Artis is fading," Renata said. "Kyra said it will be a week at most."

"And when he dies," Max said, "Leo will be the last of my family."

"Peter?"

"Is not my blood," he said. "Has never been my blood. He barely tolerated me when I was a child. I don't know why. Then again, he's not much friendlier to Leo."

"Your father's people?"

"I don't know who they are. My father's name was Ivo and he was from Normandy, but that's all I know."

"Have you looked?"

"Yes. There are very few records. It doesn't matter. Even if I found them, they aren't my family. Only Leo is."

"And me."

He hooked his arms around her knees and pulled her closer. Renata leaned into his back and rested her head on his shoulder.

"You are my heart and soul," he said. "But no one will ever know me like Leo. No one else knows what it was like to grow up as we did, strangers in our own house, a shadow hanging over us. Why did we survive when our mothers and the rest of the village didn't? Who saved us? We'll probably never know."

"*Kareshta?*"

"I told you, I remember a boy."

"But," she reminded him gently, "you were a baby—truly an infant—when the Rending happened. Perhaps your memory—"

"It's real," Max said. "He was real. And the wolves. Wolves have a scent, and it's different from dogs. I recognized it as soon as I smelled it as an adult. I was in the woods in Russia and I smelled wolves, and I knew. I knew because he kept them in the house."

Renata said nothing more. Max was as stubborn as she was. It was ridiculous to argue with him about something that had happened over two hundred years ago. It didn't matter. He'd lost his mother and father before he could remember them. He was losing his grandfather now.

"You're sad," she said.

"Yes. And... angry."

"Why?"

He ran his hands up and down her arms, stroking from her wrists to the tender skin at the curve of her elbow. "Why did he only send for us now? I sent him a letter when we mated. Leo sent his father a letter when he mated with Kyra. He's sent Artis a letter every time we've moved posts. There was never a response. But now he calls us back for this? To watch him die?"

"There are songs," Renata said. "Songs for the dying. For those who are ready to return to our fathers. Think about how many scribes have lived without those songs at the end of their lives. For thousands of years they have been part of our passage, but so many missed them. Perhaps Artis overcame his fear of the past so he could leave the earth as his ancestors did."

"Artis isn't afraid of anything." Max's voice hardened. "But I do think you're right. He didn't send for me and Leo. He sent for you. For Kyra."

"Max, that's not what I meant."

"No? It makes sense." He closed his eyes and lay back, settling into the curve of her body. "If I were him, I'd call for you too. You're a much prettier view."

"Max—"

"Can we not talk about it?" He closed his eyes and turned them toward the sun. "For a while, can we just be?"

She took a deep breath and hugged him tighter. "Yes."

KYRA WALKED UP THE STAIRS, carrying a tray of bread and meat she'd bought in the village the day before. She could hear the rhythmic ticking of a grandfather clock in the hall and muttering from the bedroom she and Leo shared. She tapped on the bottom of the door with her foot.

"What?" Leo called. He sounded cross.

"It's me. I brought some food." Leo hadn't come into the house for lunch. He'd been trimming hooves with his father that morning, then helping with the afternoon milking, then working on an outdoor water tap Artis had mentioned was leaking.

He opened the door with a frown and a smudge of dirt across his forehead. "Kyra, you shouldn't be..." He grabbed the tray. "Everything up here is a mess."

"You need to eat something."

"I'm not very hungry." He set the tray in the window seat and turned back around. "Sorry."

She stepped into the bedroom to see boxes stacked in the corner and odds and ends spread on the floor. There were books, a painted shield, and a wooden sword. A pine box was cracked open with sea glass spilling out. Papers and more books. A few clothes and an instrument that looked like a round guitar.

So many small swords. It appeared as if wooden swords and daggers were the only toys allowed.

Leo shoved some of them to the side as he walked back to the door. "Be careful."

"What are you doing?" she asked.

"Since my father refuses to say more than a dozen words to me, I thought I'd go through the things I had in storage here. I have some things..." He glanced at her. Glanced at his feet. "Some things I thought we might want for... the future."

Kyra sat on the edge of the bed and watched him shove the clutter into semiorganized piles. His eyes were sad even though he tried to put on a cheerful face. Her mate was confused. For the thousandth time, she wished she could do more to comfort him. Ava was teaching her the songs she would need for the mating ritual, but it had been a slow process. Until then, there was no magical comfort she could offer.

"Did you tell your grandfather?" she asked.

Leo paused what he was doing and walked over. He knelt at her feet and spread her knees so he could lean into her. "No. I thought about it. But I haven't told anyone, not even Max." He spread his hand over her belly and kissed the space between her breasts. "You said you weren't sure you wanted them to know."

"Only at the beginning, but we're past the most uncertain time. It's your family. It's up to you. Would the idea of a great-grandchild be a comfort to Artis or a burden? He is dying; I'm sure of it. Even his soul-voice is quiet."

"Children were never very interesting to my grandfather," Leo said. "We were annoyances until we could hold a sword and help on the farm. So I don't think he would care either way."

"I think you're not giving him enough credit."

"Trust me, I am. Artis isn't a soft man. He talks more than Peter, but he didn't kiss our bruises when we were children. Usually he was the one administering them."

"*What?*"

"With a sword." He kicked his foot out at a stack of wooden swords. "Usually with the back of a sword. Or an ax. He preferred fighting with an ax." Leo took a deep breath and let it out slowly. "I don't know what kind of father I will be, Kyra. I will have to ask Malachi many questions. He had an excellent father."

Kyra's heart was full to bursting. The fact that Leo doubted what kind of father he would be tore her heart in two.

"You will be the best father." She ran her fingers through Leo's thick blond hair as he laid his head in her lap. "Even better than Malachi. I do not know a more caring, gentle, and thoughtful man in the world."

"Do you think so?" He arched into her hand. "What if I close up like Peter? Maybe he was a good father before my mother died. Do you think Artis was a good father?"

"I know he loved your mother and your aunt very much."

Leo looked up at her. "Did he talk about them?"

"A little. He said your mother and Peter decided to get married even though Peter hardly spoke. He didn't even know they liked each other."

Leo said, "That sounds right for my father."

"And that Max's parents, Stasya and Ivo, were wildly in love and wildly suited and wildly..."

"Wild?" Leo said. "Well, that explains Max."

"And that they were *reshon*. Like us."

A slow smile spread over Leo's face, and he slid his arms around her bottom. He opened his mouth and sank his teeth into the soft flesh of her thigh. He reached down to her ankles and tickled the skin there before he lifted her long skirt, shoving it up to reveal her legs. "You're wearing too many clothes, mate of mine."

She whispered, "Artis is downstairs."

"Is he sleeping?"

"Yes, but—"

"Don't be shy." Leo stood and went to latch the hook on the door. Then he walked back to the bed and lifted her, tossing her higher on the pillows. "Didn't you say I needed to eat something?"

She felt her face heat up. Would she ever become accustomed to his teasing? "This wasn't what I had in mind."

"No, but you have to admit"—he stripped off his shirt and reached for her skirt—"my idea is much, much better."

CHAPTER FOUR

They'd been in Dunte for three days when Max felt it pressing closer. There was a presence in the woods. An energy. He walked toward the path, only to hear Artis call his name.

"Maxim!" The old man was sitting in the garden near the wood-fired oven where Kyra had set bread to rise. "What are you doing?"

Trying to figure out what is stalking us.

No, better not to bother Artis with it. The old man had softened, that Renata had been right about, but not by much. Max usually saw his grandfather staring into the distance, sometimes leaning toward something, as if there was music in another room he couldn't quite hear.

"Just taking a walk," he said. "How are you feeling this morning?"

"Fine." The old man brought a steaming mug to his mouth. "Just fine."

Max had never been in the presence of an Irin scribe or singer who was peacefully passing into the heavens. He didn't know if it was normal for them to look so healthy. Artis was as formidable as Max remembered, if slightly more distractible. Throughout Max's childhood, it had been Artis who had corralled them and made them practice their letters and books. It had been Artis who had taught them their music lessons. Artis had made them pick up their first sword.

> *Never turn your back on an enemy.*
> *Plan your path through a room as soon as you enter.*
> *Always have a way out.*
> *Don't watch an opponent's feet, watch their eyes.*
> *With Grigori, you must always fight to kill, for they will*
>   *kill you.*
> *They will kill you. They will kill your cousin. They will*
>   *kill us.*

A thousand lessons of war but none about family or friendship. Max didn't know how to relate to his grandfather in any familiar way. He strolled over to Artis. "What did you do with your ax?"

"Do you want it?" Artis asked. "It's in the armory."

The armory was a reinforced section of the barn, unassuming unless you were looking for it. It looked like a storage room unless you knew what lever to pull.

"I don't want it," Max said. "There is little use for war-axes these days. They're a bit conspicuous in urban environments."

Artis shrugged. "Well, now you know why I'm ready to die."

A rebellious shout tried to work its way out of Max's throat. "Why don't you care?"

"If you lost your Renata, you wouldn't be asking me that question."

Max knew he was right. He was just angry about it. "Then tell me why you called us here."

"Because you didn't return on your own." Artis frowned. "We waited for months for you to bring your mates to meet us. You never did."

"Why would we come where we are not welcome?"

"What are you talking about?" the old man scoffed. "This is your home. You think you need an invitation to come home? I didn't raise you to be stupid, Maxim."

"You didn't raise me to be anything. You trained a little soldier. That's all we ever were to you."

Artis's face froze.

"Be honest in your death, even if you never spoke the truth in life." Max stepped closer. "You wish we'd died with our mothers because *then* you could have mourned in peace. Or killed yourself and gone to be with them. But no, you had two small children to care for—children you didn't want—and you had to raise them. Well, you did. You raised us to be soldiers, and the world put us to use. Why do you expect us to be something we're not?"

"You have mates now," Artis said. "You should understand."

"Understand what?" Max threw up his hands. "That we were enough to stay alive for but not enough to love?" He pointed at the house and dropped his voice. "Kyra is with child. Did you know that? They think we don't know. They haven't told anyone, but Renata knew the day Kyra did. And instead of being filled with joy at such a blessing, Leo *worries*. I can see it in his face. He worries he won't be a good father because he didn't learn from his own family." Max rapped his chest with his fist. "Do you know how angry that makes me?"

Artis said nothing.

Max continued. "That man is the kindest person I have ever known in my life, and I'm not saying that because he's my cousin. He is the most purely good person I have ever met. And he is worried about loving his own child because of you and Peter."

Artis's face fell. "We did our duty. We gave you—"

"*Nothing*," Max spit out. "You trained soldiers, but you gave us nothing else. Why would we come here and bring the ones we love to a place of duty and pain? You resented us, and we felt it every moment of our childhoods."

Some unknown emotion flickered in Artis's eyes, but he quickly snuffed it out. "Do you want my ax or not?"

"I don't want your ax."

"Fine." Artis stood. "But you should take your father's sword from the armory before you go. I doubt you'll be coming back when I'm dead."

Max started. "You have my father's sword?"

"Someone in the Riga house found it and sent pictures to Peter. He kept it for you. It's clean and oiled. Peter made a new scabbard for it, but you don't have to keep it. It might not be to your taste."

"Fine." He glanced at the woods. "I need to go." He started down the path, only to stop when he heard Artis's voice.

"There's something in the woods."

Max stopped and turned. "What do you feel?"

"I feel... age. If that makes sense. Something immense and old."

"Malevolent?"

"No." The old man shook his head. "I don't think so."

It was the same feeling Max had. He didn't know what it meant, but he was going to find out.

PETER WAS STANDING in front of the forge when Leo walked in. His father's body was dripping with sweat from the fire as he held a bent horseshoe with heavy tongs. The metal glowed red-hot before Peter pulled it out and turned, placing it on the anvil.

Peter knew Leo was there. He knew the moment anyone set foot in his shop. He didn't look up or acknowledge him in any way. The smith grabbed a hammer hanging from a wooden rack and beat on the shoe, shaping it so it could be useful again.

That's what my childhood was.

Heat followed by shaping. Max and Leo were pushed to the maximum of their endurance and then pushed again. The scribes who trained them in Riga only taught them when they were at the end of their endurance. When they were malleable. Especially Max. Max had been more rebellious than Leo.

Leo had always wanted to please. He would have taken instruction just to make his father happy, but that wasn't how it was done.

Once upon a time, when their world was not filled with raw, wounded soldiers, Leo and Max would have gone to a proper scribe academy at age thirteen. They would have learned every facet of Irin life, from preserving manuscripts to magic useful for the family. They would have been taught the customs and spells to care for a mate and children, along with those for fighting, weapons, and building *talesm*. They would have had a true education from elders and soldiers and fathers and healers.

Instead, they'd been thrown into the fire and shaped to be weapons.

You're going to be a father.

Leo had frozen. He didn't know what to do. He was still trying to understand what it meant to be a mate; he didn't know anything about being a father. Then the look in Kyra's eyes had gutted him.

You don't want—
    I do. I didn't expect it so soon. Most Irin don't conceive—
    Without magic. I know. The same thing happened to Ava and Malachi.
I know we weren't trying, but—
    Kyra, I am happy. I promise I am.

What he didn't tell her was how scared he was. How the thought of a small, vulnerable child in their world made him freeze. It was hard enough being an uncle to Malachi's children. His own and Kyra's? Terrifying.

Leo sat on a pine stump his father used for shaping metal. There were hammered divots in the top. It wasn't the stump his father had used when he was a child. Pine didn't last long, and Leo had been alive for over two hundred years. He'd spent the first sixty training with his father, his grandfather, and the scribes in Riga before being presented to the Watchers' Council as a full-fledged warrior. The council traditionally didn't take scribes trained for less than a hundred years.

They'd taken Leo and Max at sixty.

Leo knew war. He knew fighting. He knew nothing about children.

Some nights in Istanbul, dark dreams would taunt him—dreams of screaming and fire—and he would wake up covered with sweat. He'd go to the courtyard, waiting under Matti and Geron's window, tracing *talesm* on his temples until he could hear every heartbeat in the house. Until he could hear their inhalations and snores. He would listen for a few minutes—wait for the pounding in his chest to pass—before he could go back to sleep.

They were so small and vulnerable.

The child in Kyra, his child, was even smaller. Only a few months old, it was barely the size of an apricot. Kyra had told him that. She had looked it up online, excited about when she would be able to hear the baby and what the baby's mind would sound like, and all Leo could think about was how would he be able to sleep knowing that his mate carried new life and he could not guard her every moment of the day.

And then he wondered how he could possibly be the kind of father his child would need when he knew nothing about having a family.

He watched his father quench the horseshoe and hang it on a bar near the forge. Peter hung the hammer and put the tongs on a rack. He was wearing a long-sleeved shirt that fully covered him. Scars and burns on *talesm* were regrettable and often damaged the magical armor their tattoos provided. Wearing protective clothing, even in the heat, was practical.

Peter was nothing if not practical.

"Did you want me?" Leo asked the silent man. "When my mother became pregnant, was it an accident or was it purposeful?"

Peter frowned. "Why would you ask that?"

"Did you want me?"

He pulled off the heavy leather gloves that covered his forearms. "We petitioned Uriel with songs and prayers for three years before your mother became pregnant."

"So you wanted me."

"I answered you."

Leo crossed his arms. The fire was still going, and trails of sweat dripped down the center of his back. "Kyra is expecting a child."

Peter, as Leo had done, froze. His eyes went wide and darted to the door. "Who is with her?"

"Renata."

Peter's posture relaxed, but only a little. "You should not have flown in an airplane to get here," he said.

"The healer assured her it wouldn't be a problem."

"You should drive back." His eyes kept going to the door.

"She's safe here," Leo said. "Do you think she isn't? Are there Grigori in the village I should know about?"

His father's spine straightened and he pulled his shoulders back. "No."

"There are no Grigori?"

"Why are you trying to provoke me, Leontios?"

"I don't know." He took a deep breath. "No, I do know. I'm angry."

"Why?"

"Because I don't understand you. And I should know what to do for her, what to do for this child. But I know none of those things because you weren't a father to me."

Peter started organizing the shop. Tongs on one wall. Hammers on another. Forging hammers. Chasing hammers. "I do not know what you want from me."

"I don't know either. Maybe nothing. Maybe some sign that..." Leo didn't hope Peter would fill the gap in conversation. "Will you at least tell me about my mother?"

Peter dropped the tongs he'd picked up. They clattered to the stones that covered the smithy, and the violent noise filled the space between father and son.

Leo had never once asked his father about his mother. Some childish instinct had warned against it. From the desolate, dead look in Peter's eyes, Leo knew that instinct had been correct.

Peter's eyes stayed on the floor, staring at the tongs he'd dropped. "I killed them all. The Grigori who came to the farm. They were still in the house." It sounded as if a voice were speaking from the grave. "I killed them all, but I couldn't find you. There was only dust."

From the little bit Artis had told Leo and Max, he knew their parents had shared a farm outside Vilnius in Lithuania. Peter had been away, trading in the city. For years, everyone had thought Peter was dead because he'd disappeared after the Rending. There was no reason for Peter to have believed Max and Leo had survived. Irin bodies dissolved at death. They left no trace but a fine gold dust.

Leo's father was utterly still, a towering bulk of muscle and *talesm* with hair only slightly greyed at the temples. He was a powerful man, but in that moment, Leo thought if he touched him —if he even came near—Peter would crumble.

"I went... a bit mad when I lost Lauma." His voice was barely above a whisper. "When I lost you."

"You didn't lose me."

Peter looked up to meet Leo's eyes. "I did."

Leo felt his throat tighten, because he realized his father was right. In that shattered moment, Peter had lost everything. Even though his son had survived, he didn't know it. He hadn't known it for seven long years.

"You got me back," Leo said softly. "Wasn't there any joy in that?"

"There was fear. I was a monster when I returned. The others didn't trust me. And you were..." Peter looked away. "You look like her. Your eyes."

183

Seven years had passed before Peter returned to find Artis. In that time, he'd scribed *talesm* down both legs and gained scars he never explained. Some of the magic had been covered over, creating thick black bands of ink over Peter's body.

Blood magic, some had whispered. *Black magic. Forbidden.*

According to the other scribes, Peter had followed no accepted code when he wreaked vengeance on those who had killed his family. He was mad. Dangerous.

"You didn't trust yourself around us," Leo said.

Peter shook his head and picked up the tongs. He set them back on the table. The forge burned behind him, throwing dark shadows despite the sun shining outside.

"I'm sorry I look like her."

"No." Peter cleared his throat. "Your eyes are what made me sane again."

The quiet confession broke Leo's heart even as it soothed the wound he'd carried since childhood.

"Those things you fear," Peter said. "Do not fear them. You have Lauma's heart. I have seen how you are with your mate. You know how to love."

His father reached into a quenching basin and picked up a dagger black from the fire. He carefully set it in a wooden brace and began to gather the polishing compounds and files he would need to finish the blade.

The conversation was over. It was the longest one they'd ever had.

MAX SPENT all day in the woods, walking old paths, surrounded by the sights and scents of childhood. He didn't find anything malevolent. He didn't find anything at all except an unexpected sense of peace.

It hadn't been all bad.

Memories washed through him as he wandered in the woods. Memories of long summers and warm fires in the winter. Catching fish and shooting arrows. Though they'd never had love or affection growing up, Max had always felt safe. And he had Leo. Leo loved him. Leo was his brighter, happier half. Leo wasn't an orphan like Max. Or at least not technically.

Max was surprised by how light his heart felt when he walked to the water. He saw Leo in the distance, sitting on the same rise where he and Renata had watched the ocean the first day they arrived.

He sat down next to his cousin and mirrored Leo, legs propped up and arms wrapped loosely around his knees. His cousin was staring at the ocean. The tide was coming in, teasing the shorebirds with spray and scattering the gulls that hopped around the rocks.

"Kyra is with child," Leo said into the wind.

"I know."

"I suspected you did."

"Everything is well?"

"Yes. She's very healthy. She spoke to Orsala in Cappadocia and a human doctor in Istanbul. She's gaining weight, but she needed to. The doctor said she was too thin."

"Good."

They stared in silence at the waves for a few minutes. "Orsala said that mixed Irin and Grigori couples are more likely to have children," Leo said. "That's why—"

"Ava and Malachi were surprised by the twins?"

"Yes."

Max said, "So was this a surprise?"

"Yes."

He threw his arm around Leo. "Blessings on you and your mate, brother. I would rejoice in any of my brothers expecting a child, but yours is a double blessing. A triple one. I am so happy for you."

Leo turned to Max, and his eyes were shining. "Will you write your blessing and ward on the baby when it comes? I know your father's blessing lies on me. And my father's on you. We're only cousins—"

"We're brothers," Max said. "And I will protect your child as I would my own. I will write my ward on the baby, Leo. And I'll love him. Or her. Maybe you'll get lucky like Malachi and get one of each."

Leo finally smiled. "There is only one heartbeat. I can hear it."

The quiet joy on his brother's face soothed Max's heart. "Can you?"

Leo nodded. "Sometimes at night I wake up and... I'm afraid. But the past few weeks, I've been able to hear the heartbeat if I focus. It lets me sleep again."

"That's good."

"And Kyra amazes me. She is so calm. She called her brother last week, and she said Kostas was crying over the phone. Happiness. He no longer wants to kill me most days."

"Greeks are more emotional than we stoic Baltic men." Max nudged his shoulder. "It's better, I think, to be like that."

Leo nodded. "I told my father."

"What did he say?" Max paused. "Wrong question. Did he say anything at all?"

"He did." Leo glanced over his shoulder toward the farm in the distance. "He was afraid for us. Worried about Kyra's safety. I think I might finally... not understand him. Or maybe I understand him a little. And maybe that's all I need."

Max wanted to shout that Leo deserved a father who loved him and showed it, but that wasn't what Leo needed. His issues with Peter were his own, and Max had no illusions that change would come quickly. If Leo felt more at ease with his father, that was all Max could hope for.

"I'm glad," he said. "You're going to make a wonderful father, Leo."

"Do you think so?" Insecurity was written all over his face.

"I know you will. You've always taken care of me, and I'm not nearly as cute as your baby will be."

Leo smiled. "I think it will look like Kyra. Grigori genes are strong."

You're strong. So much stronger than me to remain open and accepting of others and expect so little for yourself. Max felt a fierce wave of love for his brother. "Your child will have so many people who love him, Leo. So many. It won't be like it was with us. I promise you that."

"I know." Leo brushed the back of his hand over his eyes. "I know that, but thank you for telling me."

Max sat quietly for a few moments until he felt it again. There was a presence in the woods. An energy that felt foreign. It wasn't Grigori. It wasn't one of the Fallen. It wasn't…

"Do you feel it?" Leo asked quietly. "In the woods?"

"Do you know what it is?"

"I've been thinking… it is Death." Leo took a deep breath. "Like in Vienna."

"Yes." Max tried to remember what the angel of death had felt like, but his memories of that day were jumbled. "I think you're right."

Leo nodded. "This feels a little bit like that."

"So not a bad thing?"

"No. Artis is ready."

"I can't imagine welcoming death. Can you?"

"Of course not," Leo said. "We've just begun to live."

They sat by the water until the sun went down. They didn't speak anymore, but if there was one lesson Max had learned from his grandfather and his uncle, it was this: some moments were beyond words.

CHAPTER FIVE

"What is it?" Kyra asked. "Is it for the kitchen?"

The basket was tangled with ropes and looked like it was made from the grasses by the beach. Parts of it were worn with age, and parts of it were green from repair.

"No." Artis picked up the hook and lifted it. "It's a cradle."

Of *course* it was. Kyra felt a smile spreading on her lips. "A basket cradle."

Sturdy rope suspended the finely woven basket, and colorful strings and trinkets were hung on the outside and the base. It was oblong and quite long, large enough for a toddler.

"I don't know what you use in the south, but we liked these kind of cradles when we had babies," Artis said. "You could put a hook anywhere in the house but also take it outside and hang it from a tree. They're light because the basket is made from grass, not branches. One of the women in the village patched the places that were weak. It's watertight too, as long as you let the grasses swell up before you put the baby in. Evelina used one like this and tied the ropes to the rocks by the stream. The water put the girls to sleep."

"So clever."

"You'll be able to use it for your baby. If you want it."

Kyra swallowed hard. "I love it. Thank you, Artis." She fingered the colorful strings stacked with beads. There were tiny bells and decorative metal pieces hanging all around the basket. When the wind blew, they would act like little wind chimes, tinkling in the breeze. "I will enjoy taking it out to the garden, and I'll make sure Leo puts a hook from the ceiling in the house."

"This was his mother's."

"Then I like it even more." Kyra smiled at Artis, and the old man almost—almost!—smiled back.

"It's sturdy." He lowered the cradle to the floor and bundled the ropes inside. "We had big babies, Evelina and me."

"I consider myself warned."

When Leo had told his grandfather that Kyra was having a baby, the old man hadn't said much. But he'd nodded and rocked in the old chair by the fire, and Kyra didn't think she was imagining the emotion in his eyes.

Peaceful. He looked peaceful.

He'd spent the next two days opening cedar trunks with Leo and Max, pulling out old things that had belonged to their family. A set of silver spoons. Blankets knitted by Evelina and her mother. Wooden cups and small toys that had belonged to Lauma and Stasya. Artis had kept it all hidden away.

Renata and Kyra had sorted through the treasures, putting some things back in storage and packing others. The basket cradle, Kyra definitely wanted to take.

"Leo is talking about driving back," Kyra said. "We can't take all these things on the plane."

"You shouldn't be flying," Artis said. "A car would be better."

"It's three days of driving. Probably four or five."

"What is a few days?" Artis shrugged. "You have time."

"I suppose you're right." She put a hand on his forearm.

At Renata's suggestion, she was trying to touch Artis more. Irin scribes and singers needed contact with each other. They were not designed to be a solitary race. It was possible it had been over two hundred years since an Irina had laid hands on either Peter or Artis, which would leave the men so severely out of balance it was detrimental to their health. Just like she needed Leo to ground her energy, Leo needed her to balance and lift him.

"Can you feel what is in the woods?" Artis asked her. "Do you fear it?"

"Fear it?" Kyra shook her head. "If it is Azril, he is familiar to me."

She hadn't been surprised to feel Azril's presence around the house. It had grown stronger every day, but it did not frighten her. The angel of death was neither Fallen nor Forgiven. He played by neither set of rules but lived in a limbic space between the heavenly and earthly realm. And if her father Barak had anything like friends, Azril had been one.

"He is familiar?"

"He often visited my father," Kyra said. "I do not fear him. He was always gentle with my sisters."

Artis's eyes were wide. "I see."

"Are you afraid?" Kyra laid a hand on her belly. "Or reluctant now? I told Leo I didn't want to tell you about the baby because I wasn't sure if you would feel obligated."

"My great-grandchild will be well protected. Of that I have no doubt. I am ready." He took a deep breath and slowly released it. "I have been ready for hundreds of years."

She nodded. "I promise, if you welcome him, he will be kind to you."

"I will remember that." He laid a tentative hand on Kyra's shoulder. "Thank you, daughter."

"You're welcome." She looked at the cradle. "And thank you. I will treasure it."

MAX AND RENATA sat in the woods, perched on logs in the middle of a ring of trees where the strange presence felt strongest.

"What are we doing here?" Renata asked. She wasn't afraid, but she was uncomfortable. Something about waiting for death scraped on her nerves. Death was a thief, stealing her family from her. It had stolen Max's mother and father, stolen any kind of childhood from him.

"Wait," he said. "Just wait."

When her mate had become a Zen master of calm was a mystery to Renata. They had been at the farm for seven days, having one-sided conversations with Artis and Peter, milking cows, and taking care of repairs. Kyra had baked enough bread to feed a small village, and Renata had spent time caring for the animals, which was soothing. Leo sat in the smithy with his silent father, and Max had spent most of the week walking through the woods.

"I can hear you thinking," Max said. "You need to quiet your mind."

"I can't quiet my mind."

"Then sing something," he said. "Sing a song that Azril might like."

"Why do you want to meet him so much? Do you have a death wish I need to know about?"

Max chuckled. "Not at all." He put his arm around her and grabbed a handful of her backside. "I have too much living to do right now."

"Then why—"

"I have a theory," Max said. "And it has to do with two baby boys left after a massacre. Boys that Death didn't take when he came for their mothers. Boys who disappeared for some time and then reappeared, completely unharmed, at a scribe house near their destroyed home."

Renata's eyes went wide. "You think Azril is the boy you remember?"

Max's eyes danced. "I don't know. But he would have been

there, wouldn't he? To carry their souls to heaven. He would have been with them. He would have seen us and… I don't know. Done something."

She couldn't ask why knowing mattered so much to him. She had books of history written in her heart. She knew every story about her birth and childhood. The roots of her family were dug so deep that even when the tree had been chopped at the base, it had sprung up again in her, too strong for death to kill it.

Max's roots had been ripped out and never truly replanted.

So Renata did the only thing she could do. She opened her mouth and sang a song to welcome Death.

> *My soul is ready*
> *I am ready to fly.*
> *Fly to the heavens*
> *where my ancestors rest.*
> *My soul is ready*
> *to take your hand.*
> *Death, where do you stay?*
> *Bringer of peace, where do you rest?*
> *Old friend, I am waiting for you.*
> *You visit the king in his bed of gold*
> *and the beggar you treat the same.*
> *Full welcome are you,*
> *friend to singer and scribe.*
> *Death, come swiftly for I am in wait.*

As Renata sang in the Old Language, she felt the air stir around her. She blinked and saw a man who was not a man appear in the middle of the clearing. He was beautiful and his face was unlined, though the silver eyes that watched them through thick black lashes bore the weight and bearing of eternity.

Far from a celestial being, he seemed to grow from the earth. He sat on the ground. His face was unlined, with light brown skin and Baltic features as familiar as Max's. He was shrouded in a cloak made of fine bark and grass, but when he moved, it sounded to Renata like a bird taking flight. An eight-pointed star shone on his forehead. His presence was immense, though he appeared no taller than Max.

"You're Azril," Max said. "But you're not the boy."

The angel smiled. *No.*

The words didn't leave the creature's mouth, but he spoke them into their minds. Renata knew Max had heard the same voice, because his shoulders slumped in disappointment.

Wait. The angel raised his hand. *Wait.*

They waited for what could have been minutes or hours. Renata had lost all sense of time and space as she stared at Death in corporeal form. "You took them all," she said quietly.

He nodded. *It is my purpose.*

"Did it hurt?"

This earthly realm offers pain, but my touch is gentle. Do not fear me. When I come for you, I will be a welcome friend.

"I may have sung the song," she said. "But I'm not ready. Not nearly ready. So don't remember where I live, do you hear me?"

Azril smiled, and a laughing voice echoed in her mind. *I never forget anything, but I'll do my best to misplace you. Will that do?*

Max grabbed her hand. "That will do."

In the distance, Renata heard footsteps rustling through the forest. Leo's voice was the first thing she recognized.

"...don't like it when he just shows up like this."

"I didn't call him this time."

"*This* time? You mean the other times you *did* call him?"

"Leo, he's young! I think he gets lonely."

"That's not true." A clear voice rang through the woods. "I don't get lonely."

Leo, Kyra, and a very sullen-looking Vasu stepped into the clearing in the middle of the pines.

Max immediately tried to stand, but Renata kept him next to her.

Vasu walked into the clearing and pointed at Azril. "He called me."

There are stories that need to be told, little brother.

"Why?" Vasu leaned on a tree, his arms crossed. That day, the fallen angel appeared to be little more than a teenager and entirely deserving of the sullen label Kyra had given him. His hair was thick and black with gold streaks woven through it. He was dressed entirely in black and looked far more like an angel of death than the wild creature in the middle of the wood.

Tell them.

"Does it matter now?"

That is not for you to decide. Tell them because they want to know. Azril looked at Kyra. *And she needs to hear it.*

Vasu huffed out a breath. "I don't know where to start."

Then I will start and you will finish. Azril stared directly at Max. *Picture a forest very much like this one.*

Max closed his eyes, and Azril's voice flowed over them, lulling Renata into a kind of trance.

She hid you in the forest while her mate fought them back. They had already killed her twin. She felt her soul tear in half, but she was determined. Though she called out for my mercy, she was adamant. They could not have the children too.

Max said, "My mother. You're talking about my mother in the forest."

I was there to take their hands, son of Leoc. If you reach very far, you might find their last moments. Your blood would allow it, but do not look for them; remember their bravery. Your father fought so your mother could escape with the babes. She heard them in the woods. I saw them run after her.

"But you did nothing?" Leo said.

Azril cocked his head. *It is not for me to intervene. That is not my purpose.*

"But you did intervene!" Vasu shouted. "You and Barak both. You called him and he came, and was that His will? Was it, Azril?"

Renata felt the chill in her bones as Max gripped her hand. Barak? What did Kyra's Fallen father have to do with this?

Azril continued as if he'd heard nothing.

She lay on the forest floor and I came to her. She was angry and afraid. "You cannot take them," she told me when I took her hand. "They are not for you."

"She hid us in the forest," Leo said.

In a cradle made of grass.

"A basket cradle," Kyra said. "Like Artis gave to me."

She put a spell over the babies. You slept for many hours.

"And then my father found them," Kyra said. "Didn't he? Vasu said you called him."

I always called Barak; he listened.

Kyra reached for Leo's hand. "He and the wolves came; he's the one who saved Max and Leo. The boy with the golden eyes."

His true visage would have been too frightening.

"But why?" Leo asked.

I could not take the children. They were not for me.

Max spoke in a hoarse voice. "But why did he save *us*? Hundreds of children died in the Rending. Maybe thousands. What were we to him?"

Vasu cocked his head and finally spoke. "The Rending *offended* Barak. He saw the world in a state of balance, and the massacre disrupted it. He withdrew from the world after it happened, killed any of his sons who had taken part. He let others take his territory. Eventually he even let his children think he was dead." Vasu nodded at Max. "That was your doing. Both of you."

"You think two Irin babies influenced the course of an archangel's history?" Leo said. "You give us too much credit, Vasu."

"Your blood mixed with his," Vasu said. "It's always the beginning of the end for us. Once we cross into the terrestrial realm in that way, we begin to *feel* things." Vasu shivered. "That's why I avoid Forgiven children as much as possible."

Leo said, "What do you mean, our blood mixed?"

"You had a wound on your leg from one of the wolves," Vasu said. "Barak kicked the wolf back and healed the cut with his blood because it had been his animal that harmed you."

"And that was it?" Max asked. "Barak gave up his power on earth because Leo had a cut on his leg?"

Vasu frowned. "Blood has power, scribe. Barak gave his power to the powerless. He saved the children of his enemies. In doing that, he altered his history and your own. He tied your line together with his. If you think any of this is an accident, then you haven't been paying attention." And with that, Vasu blinked out of sight.

Leo, Kyra, Renata, and Max were left in the forest with Azril, whose eyes rested on Kyra.

She walked over and sat on the ground in front of Death, crossing her legs and putting her hands on her belly.

Leo started forward. "Kyra, don't." He reached out but let his hand fall when he saw the angel pass a hand over his mate's head in a caress as maternal as any human or Irina mother.

Kyra smiled. "Hello, Azril."

Daughter, you touch eternity.

"Do you know?" Kyra asked. "Can you see it?"

Yes. The joy in his voice was incandescent. The air around them shimmered with it. *Your child will be blessed in this realm and the next.*

"Thank you, Azril."

It is good to see you so happy.

"It is good to see you."

The shining note that echoed in Renata's mind was nothing like a voice, though she knew it came from the angel. It was a pealing bell and an exuberant birdsong. A pure expression of joy so acute it made her eyes water.

Azril spoke to Renata. *Thank you for calling me. Your song honors your mother.*

"Thank you."

Max squeezed her hand. "It's been you in the forest this week, hasn't it?"

I know the old one waits for me.

"Will you come when he's ready?" Leo asked.

Of course. Azril began to fade from view. *I will always come.*

LEO LAY AWAKE THAT NIGHT, staring at the ceiling. His hand rested on Kyra's belly, and he listened to the rapid heartbeat of the child in her womb. At first the pace of it had frightened him. Then the doctor assured them it was the way all babies' hearts beat. His child was healthy. According to Azril, his child would have a long and blessed life. Or at least that was what Death had told his mate. And what had he told Leo?

I could not take the children. They were not for me.

So Barak and Azril had saved two children and returned them to half-dead men who raised them without evident love or affection. They had raised warriors who went on to hunt demons and bring down angels.

Leo rolled over and watched Kyra as she slept. Her dark hair splayed over the pillow beside him, and he tucked a piece of it under his cheek, smoothing the silk between his fingers. *Reshon.* Lover. Mate. Mother. She was all things to him.

Perhaps Barak heard the echo of the Creator's will in a baby's cry. By protecting Leo and Max, Barak had saved a life that would eventually connect with his own line.

Your blood mixed with his.

Leo laid his hand on Kyra's belly again. Barak's blood. Fallen blood. Forgiven blood. They lived in this tiny child just as Jaron's blood lived in Malachi and Ava's children.

Who are we becoming?

Wiser men than Leo had tried to answer that. But maybe it came back to what Barak had believed. A world in balance. Life and death. Dark and light. One life entered the world as another life left it. He pulled Kyra closer as she slept.

"Leo?" she murmured as she tucked her face into his neck. "You all right?"

He took a deep breath and inhaled the sweet frangipani perfume she used in her hair. He ran a hand over her arm, which was growing plump and full as her body prepared for their child. His restlessness fled, and he felt a peace beyond understanding fill his soul.

"I am," he whispered. "I'm all right."

Joy could be built on pain, just as good could come from evil.

Leo finally believed that, and he slept.

EPILOGUE

A rtis stayed outside his last night on earth, staring at the stars in a night filled with music and singing. Max played the guitar while Peter played the mandolin. Leo built a fire, and Artis sat in front of it wrapped only in linen, his body in touch with the earth that had held it for so long.

Kyra sat next to him on a cushion Leo had insisted on. She fed small sticks into the fire and watched the smoke rise while Renata sang softly next to Max. She watched Artis turn his face up to the heavens. His soul was drifting before her. His expression was peaceful, and Kyra was glad.

She said, "My father used to tell his children we weren't at home here. That we had no home. But I don't think that's right."

"No?"

"No, I think we have two homes. One here and one in heaven. Why limit yourself to only one home?"

Artis turned his eyes to Leo and Max. "Do you think they will come back here after I am gone?"

"I don't know."

"They should come back to visit Peter. Bring the baby to visit Peter."

"You should tell them that."

Artis shrugged. "They will do what they want."

"You should tell them anyway."

Kyra hummed along with Renata's song. The night was cool, but Leo had draped a blanket around her shoulders. Between the blanket and the fire, Kyra was comfortable.

"What should we talk about?" she asked.

"I don't know," Artis said. "I think we have talked about everything important. Maybe that is how you know when you are ready to go."

"You will see Evelina again."

A true smile crossed Artis's face. "Yes."

"And Lauma. And Stasya and Ivo."

The old man nodded.

"I don't know if you will remember the things of this world when you are in the next. But if you do, tell them about their magnificent sons." Kyra's eyes filled with tears. "Tell Lauma and Stasya and Ivo their sons are loved and celebrated. That Leo is going to be a father and that Max has found peace."

"I will tell them."

"Tell Lauma..." Kyra cleared her throat. "Tell Lauma that even if Leo doesn't come, I will bring the baby to visit Peter. That he won't be alone."

Artis turned to her, and there were tears in his eyes. "I will tell her."

"Good." Kyra sniffed. "That's good."

"And if I see your father in the heavenly realm, what should I say to Barak?"

Kyra took a deep breath. "Tell him... thank you for saving the other half of my heart. And tell him I am happy."

THEY SLEPT OUTSIDE on makeshift pallets of blankets and straw mattresses. Renata lay on her back with Max's head on her breast, staring at the stars that dotted the sky.

"You're not sleeping," Max murmured.

"I'm not tired." She blinked when a star crossed the sky. "I'm not ready to say goodbye to him. We don't have enough elders in our world."

"We have plenty of cranky old men. We're lacking women though."

"Do you understand, Max?"

He lifted his head. "What?"

She blinked away tears. "He's leaving us. I just met him, and he's leaving us."

"He decided over a century ago how this would be. He's already fading. Would you keep him from his mate?" Max brushed a thumb over her cheek. "From his daughters? You know better than I do how he must be missing them."

She nodded.

"Then we say goodbye," he said. "It is not forever."

Renata kissed his hand. "No, not forever. But for a very long time."

"Do you remember what I said to you at Midwinter? About the thing that I feared?"

I think what I'm most afraid of in this life is that I will get to the end of it —die in battle or just from exhaustion—and have no memories of home.

She kissed him. "Do you have memories of home now?"

"I have memories of you, and that is the same thing." Max rolled to the side and tucked Renata against his body. "And Artis has memories by the hundreds. Memories of growing up here and falling in love with a beautiful and gifted singer. Memories of his mate baking the most delicious bread and his daughters rocking in a cradle by the stream. Memories of his daughters finding love and having their own children."

Renata said, "And now he has memories of his grandchildren finding love. Of a new generation being born."

Max nodded. "His life has been full, and now he is ready to leave. He would not be drifting away if the Creator didn't know he was ready."

"I know that."

"But...?"

She looked across the glowing coals of the fire to where Peter sat in vigil next to Artis's prone body.

"I'm still going to miss him."

LEO WOKE in the night to see his father watching his grandfather with the most tender expression Leo had ever seen on the man's face. He rose from his bed, covered Kyra with a heavy blanket, and walked to sit beside them.

Peter brushed a tuft of grey hair back from Artis's forehead. "I will miss him."

"I know."

"He was my teacher. Then he was my family. The only thing I had left."

Leo took a deep breath and came to a decision. "You have me and Max. And Kyra and Renata. You'll have the baby too. You have family, Father."

Peter looked at Leo for a long time. "I am sorry, Leontios."

"For what?"

Peter frowned. "You know."

Did Leo need the words? Would he demand them for his own vindication or accept what his father was offering?

Let it be, the wind whispered through the forest. *Let it be.*

"I know," Leo said. "I forgive you."

"You are stronger than I am."

Leo shook his head. "No, I don't think so."

"You are." Peter put a hand on Leo's shoulder. "I can see."

"Thank you."

Peter stretched his legs out, pointing his feet toward the fire. "I think I will tell the scribes in Riga I have need of an apprentice."

"That's a good idea."

"There is room here. The world is changing, but we always need smiths."

"Who knows?" Leo said. "The way the world is changing, the scribe house might send you a singer instead of a scribe."

Peter's eyebrows went up, but he shrugged. "As long as she can swing a hammer."

"That I might have to see." He glanced at his father. "We'll come next summer when the baby can travel. Maybe you'll have a new apprentice by then."

"Thank you." Peter's voice was barely above a whisper. "I will... expect you."

MAX AND LEO walked on either side of their grandfather, helping the fading scribe down to the beach as the sun began to rise and the morning sky turned pink. Renata walked behind them, singing the songs of the dying. Kyra walked with Peter, one of Evelina's blankets wrapped around her shoulders.

As Artis began to stumble, she saw Azril walk from the forest to meet them on the dunes where the long grass swayed.

The old scribe lay down in the sand and let out a labored breath, his eyes locked on the horizon. Leo and Max knelt beside their grandfather, supporting his back. He put a hand on both their heads, whispering in turn to each of them. He clutched their hands and looked to the sky before his eyes closed in peace. A smile touched his lips, and Kyra could see the borders between his body and his soul blur in the dawn light.

Azril looked at Kyra and smiled.

"Do you see him?" she asked Peter.

"I do." Peter's voice was choked. "Is he…?"

"That's Azril." Kyra smiled. "He's a friend." She wasn't surprised by Peter's reaction. Who expected Death to come with a gentle smile? "He's always the same. Everywhere on the earth, he has always been. The world can be cruel. Humans and angels both. But Azril isn't cruel. When your mate left this world, she took his hand and she would have known peace. I promise, Peter."

He stared at Azril. "Thank you."

"You're welcome."

Renata's voice rose as the sun did, singing high and clear in the morning mist. As she sang, Azril walked to Artis and knelt down at his feet. He reached his hand from the grass cloak and offered it.

Kyra saw Artis smile. Then the old scribe reached out, and his fading hands clutched Death's offering. The moment they touched, his body began to shimmer with a faint gold light.

The smile on Azril's face was incandescent. *Walk with me, Artis of Dunte. Your body is no longer your home.*

Artis's body dissolved in a shower of gold light and his dust rose, carried by the angel to the heavenly realm.

MAX LOADED the cradle basket in the back of the truck as Renata and Kyra debated which trunks to take and which to leave at the farm. They were already planning their visit next summer, ordering Leo around as he carted things in and out of the house.

Peter walked over to Max with a wrapped bundle under his arm.

"What is that?" Max asked.

Peter held out the bundle. "Your father's sword. Someone in Vilnius sent pictures to Riga and they sent the pictures to me. I recognized the markings on the blade and bought it. It had been in the collection of a human who did not know what the *talesm* were."

It might have been the longest sentence Max had ever heard from his uncle.

Then again, it was about weapons.

"Thank you." Max unwrapped the bundle and looked at the finely worked leather of the scabbard.

"I made the scabbard."

"It's beautiful, Peter. Thank you."

"It was dangerous to leave it with the humans," Peter said. "This was forged with very strong magic and has a silver core." He drew the sword from the scabbard with the practiced hand of an expert. "Ivo took great pride in this sword. He never said how old it was, but I would estimate fifteenth century, so it likely belonged to his father since your father was my age."

Max's eyes went wide. "You knew him."

"Yes." Peter frowned. "Ivo was my best friend."

Of course he was. The two men had loved twin sisters. They had been family. They had worked the same farm in Vilnius and written blessings for each other's children. Peter and Ivo had probably been nearly as close as Leo and Max.

In that moment, Max understood—truly understood—the magnitude of Peter's loss.

Mate. Sister. Brother. Children.

Peter had lost everything that day. The fact that he wasn't a raving monster was a miracle.

His uncle was overdue for grace. What good did it do to hold on to resentment? Nothing new or better could come from it.

Grace.

"I would like to hear more about my father when we come next summer." Max reached out his hand. "If you would be willing, Uncle."

Peter hesitated, but he took Max's outstretched hand and nodded.

"Perhaps, if you would rather not speak of it, you could write it down."

"That would be better," Peter said. "I can do that."

"Be well." Max carefully slid his father's sword back in the scabbard, brushing a hand over the protective magic bound into the sheath. He could see from the workmanship that the scabbard had taken many hours to create. "I'll... send letters about the baby when I can."

"And about yourself," Peter said. "And Renata."

"If you wish."

"Yes." Peter nodded again. "I would like that."

They loaded the rest of the truck and pulled away just after the midday meal. Max slid behind the driver's seat and reached a hand out for Renata. Kyra was already sleeping in the back seat, and Leo was listening to music on his headphones.

"Ready to go home?" Renata asked.

Max kissed her knuckles before he put the truck in gear and pulled away from the place that had been his home. A place that he hoped might become a home again.

"I'm with my family," he said. "I'm always home."

THE END

Sign up for my newsletter for more information about Rhys and Meera's book, THE SEEKER, the next book in the Irin Chronicles, coming Summer 2018. Turn the page for an exclusive preview!

PREVIEW: THE SEEKER

Houston, Texas

Rhys of Glast, only son of Edmund of Glast and Angharad the Sage, Irin scribe and archivist of Istanbul, was not impressed by the biscuits and gravy at the diner in on Kirby Drive. The biscuits were passably flaky, but the gravy tasted too much of flour and was thick enough to stand a fork in. Fortunately, the chocolate cream pie had redeemed the meal.

The waitress walked around the counter and down to Rhys's booth with a steaming pot of coffee. "Warm up?"

Rhys quickly put a hand over his mug, an edge of ash-black ink peeking from the long-sleeved linen shirt he wore. "Tea."

Her brown eyes widened. "Pardon me, sugar?"

"Tea," Rhys said again. "I'm drinking tea, not coffee."

She smiled. "That's right. Can I get you some more hot water?"

"Please. And another bag of tea."

"You got it." She walked away with a natural sway to her wide hips, dodging the server coming at her with practiced grace.

There were two waitresses working in the diner that night, the older black woman with greying hair and quick reflexes and a younger white woman Rhys suspected was just starting her job. She looked to the older woman almost constantly for cues and lingered at a table in the back corner near the toilets where a brown-haired young man smiled and flirted with her.

In addition to the waitresses there were seven other patrons. Three students who had taken over a round booth, a middle-aged couple who appeared to be quietly fighting, an older man lifting coffee to his mouth with shaking hands, and the Grigori flirting with the young waitress.

Rhys sipped his tea as he watched the Grigori. It was plain black tea, nothing like the symphony of teas he was accustomed to in Istanbul. There one could find tea blended with spices from all over the world in countless varieties and subtle variations. Love of tea had redeemed Istanbul for Rhys.

Pie was on the way to redeeming Houston.

The Grigori glanced at Rhys and opened his newspaper, pointedly ignoring the scribe who watched him. The air-conditioning blasted in the restaurant, even in the middle of the night, forcing the hot, wet air of the Bayou City to cold condensation that ran down the windows and scattered the light of the passing traffic on Kirby Drive.

The Grigori glanced up, then looked down again. Despite the air-conditioning, Rhys could see a gleam of perspiration at the man's temples.

Rhys of Glast had spent his formative years in the cool mists of Cornwall and southern England, but for some reason known only to the Creator, his entire adult career had been spent in various places that baked and steamed.

Spain. Morocco. Istanbul.

And now he was being sent to New Orleans, Louisiana by way of Houston, Texas.

Hot and hotter.

The waitress returned with a battered metal pot with a red and yellow packet wedged on the side. "You want another piece of pie?"

She motioned to the near-empty plate. "Sure didn't seem like you liked the biscuits and gravy much."

"I didn't."

The woman didn't look offended; her pink-painted mouth turned up at the corner. "More pie, Mr. Bond?"

"I beg your pardon?"

The waitress glanced over her shoulder before she turned back to Rhys. "Fancy British guy eating pie and drinking tea at two in the morning on a Wednesday night? Sitting in the corner booth with one eye on the door and the other on that flirty fella in the booth by the bathroom?" She wrote something down on her order pad. "If I didn't know you weren't carrying, I'd be worried."

Rhys sat up straighter. "Not that you're wrong, but how do you know I'm not carrying a firearm?"

The tilted smile turned into a grin. "Sugar, I've been waiting tables in Texas for thirty-five years. I know when someone's got a gun."

"Fair enough." He made a mental note not to discount the waitress.

Rhys hadn't approached the Grigori by the toilets. He'd been drawn to the diner by the scent of sandalwood that followed the half-angelic creatures—sons of the Fallen always carried the distinctive scent—but so far, the Grigori had done nothing but flirt, and that was built into its DNA. In the complicated times they lived in, that meant Rhys was forced to show restraint.

No longer could scribes hunt Grigori on sight. Though the Irin race was charged with protecting humanity from the offspring of fallen angels, recent revelations had turned black and white to countless shades of grey.

Some Grigori wrested freedom from their Fallen fathers and conquered their predatory instincts. Many of those had turned those instincts to join the Irin in their quest to rid humanity of fallen angels. Some of their sisters, the kareshta, had mated with

209

Irin scribes. Rhys's own brother-in-arms was mated to the sister of a Grigori the Istanbul scribes had once hunted.

It was all so complicated now.

"Has he done anything to concern you?" Rhys asked the waitress quietly. "The man by the bathrooms?"

"No." She lifted the empty pie plate. "Just sitting there reading his paper. He likes the blueberry and wears too much cologne. Not my type."

Rhys forced his eyes away from the Grigori. "Another piece of chocolate for me."

"Cook just put a black-bottomed pie in the case."

His mouth watered. "That sounds perfect."

"See?" She winked at him. "Knew you were my type."

Rhys couldn't help his smile.

"You be good," she said, walking back to the counter.

Rhys sometimes longed for the days when the borders between enemy and friend were clear. Only a few years ago, he could have stalked the creature waiting in the restaurant with a clean conscience; run him to the ground, pierced his neck with the silver blades he he hid, and watched Grigori dust rise to the heavens to face judgement.

It is what they deserve, a vengeful voice whispered inside him. It was the Grigori who had slain the Irina singers. It was the Grigori who had tried to wipe out their race. It was the Grigori—

No.

That wasn't their world now. Rhys dunked the tea bag into the silver pot. That would never be their world again. Their world demanded forgiveness. It required reconciliation, both within their race between the Irin who hunted and the Irina who hid, and outside their race between the Irin and Grigori who pursued a peaceful life.

So Rhys waited for his tea to steep.

And he watched.

At four in the morning, the air outside the dinner was still muggy. Rhys toyed with the end of a cinnamon toothpick as he watched the entrance of the diner from the car he'd rented at the airport. His phone was on speaker, and his brother Maxim was speaking.

"The Houston scribe house and the New Orleans house are combined under one watcher. It's a situation that's persisted despite complaints from New Orleans, but the American Watcher's council is unconvinced that New Orleans needs a stronger presence."

Rhys said, "It's a large tourist destination." Grigori liked to feed on tourists.

"True. But as far as anyone can tell, attacks are surprisingly low. Houston has more. Larger population, bigger house."

Rhys pulled the toothpick from between his lips. "Fallen presence?"

"The closest known Fallen stronghold is in St. Louis. There are always minor angels about, but Bozidar is the closest known archangel and he resides in and around St. Louis. Prior to his arrival around two hundred years ago, there hadn't been a significant Fallen presence in North America for four hundred years because of the Native Irin presence."

And by Irin, Max meant what their people had once been. Not the fractured and suspicious people they were now. The Native Irin of North America were legend in Rhys's world, a vibrant and powerful society of warrior scribes and singers descended from Uriel, the oldest and wisest of the Forgiven angels. Renowned for their long lives and prowess in battle, they had routed the archangel Nalu and all his cadre eight hundred years before, leading to a golden age of Irin peace that lasted for roughly five hundred years.

But with European expansion into North America, new Grigori and new Fallen came, breaking the rule of the Native Irin.

Rhys said, "North America didn't escape the Rending."

"Nowhere did," Max said. "But they had already been weakened by the American Civil War. By the time the Rending happened, many Irin communities were already scattered, more stories than actual presence."

"So what you're saying is it's entirely possible she was already in hiding and lived."

Maxim didn't respond. Rhys frowned and tore his eyes away from the diner entrance to make sure they still had a connection.

"Max? Are you there?"

"I am. According to Sari's contact, the Wolf is definitely still living. And it's likely somewhere in Louisiana. If we can find her—"

"We might be one step closer to restoring Irina status."

Max said, "The Irina need to relearn martial magic if they want a chance at regaining their place in Vienna."

The Rending, the massive global Grigori attack that had killed eighty percent of Irin women and children hadn't happened out of nowhere. The Irina had spent centuries focusing on creative, artistic, and scientific magic, letting their focus drift to peaceful pursuits while Irin scribes gained more and more battle prowess. Battle had become men's work, far beneath Irina pursuits. It had left the Irina vulnerable to attack.

Two hundred years after the Rending, most surviving Irina were reluctant to leave the havens where they'd hidden. The Elder Council in Vienna was the governing body of the Irin people, financing the scribe houses and protecting the secrecy of the Irin race in the human world. Since the Rending, the council was made of old men reluctant to part with their power.

Damien and Sari, former watchers in Istanbul, had taken over the warrior training center in the Czech Republic. They were desperate to rediscover the martial spells Irina had once sung in battle. Songs that had once destroyed angels had been lost to time, since Irina libraries existed only in Irina singers themselves. Irina librarians were knowledge in human form. Walking encyclopedias of magic, able to recall complex spells from memories trained since birth. They did not write magic down, believing that the delivery and emotion behind oral preservation were as essential as the spells themselves.

It was a stubborn ideology that drove Rhys mad.

He was a scribe of Gabriel's blood, trained to preserve knowledge and copy any manuscript with precision, gifted in tattooing intricate magic on his body. Rhys's tattoos, his talesm, started on his left wrist, wrapped around his arm and up his shoulder, down his chest, torso, and right arm, covering his body from the tops of his thighs to his neck. Only the space over his heart was bare, waiting for the mating mark he was half-convinced would never come.

His talesm were not only a magical armor, but a personal history. Every scribe was trained to preserve knowledge for future Irin generations in the most efficient and sensible way: writing.

"This Wolf," Rhys asked, "is she a librarian?"

"Better," Max said.

Rhys rolled his eyes. At this point in their history, there was nothing more valuable than an Irina librarian. "So what is she?"

"She's the sister of the Serpent."

Rhys blinked. "You can't be serious."

"I am."

"They were both killed."

"No. Ulakabiche died in battle, but his sister didn't. Atawakabiche lives. At least according to Sari's contact."

"And not once in nearly three hundred years has she revealed herself to her sisters?"

Max sighed. "Don't ask me, Rhys. You're the archivist. That's why Damien sent you on this job. Sort out truth from legend, talk to this woman in New Orleans, and find out if the Wolf is still living. She and her brother were the most feared Irin warriors in North America. Atawakabiche's magic destroyed an archangel without the use of a heavenly blade. If she exists, she could change everything."

Rhys considered what he knew:

Atawakabiche, the Tattooed Wolf, had been a legendary and powerful leader.

There was no trusted record of her death, only rumors.

Native Irina in the Southern United States had withdrawn long before the Rending.

There was a surprising lack of Grigori attacks in New Orleans, despite a ready and available stream of tourists.

Sari was the opposite of a fool.

Damien trusted her implicitly.

"Who is Sari's contact?" Rhys asked.

"An Irina named Meera. She'll meet you in New Orleans in three days. Go to Jackson Square on Saturday morning and she'll find you."

Rhys groaned. "She wants to meet me among the biggest tourist traffic in New Orleans on Saturday morning? Is she serious?"

"I don't make the decisions here, brother. I'm passing along information. Be there by nine."

"In the morning?" Rhys curled his lip. He was a night owl.

"Nine in the morning, my friend. Be there."

Rhys's eyes locked on the dark-haired man walking out of the diner with a woman on his arm. It was the Grigori and the young waitress. He opened his car door and spit the toothpick on the ground. "Max, I have to go. I'll call you when I get on the road."

"What are you doing?"

Rhys slid his hand into his pocket, his fingers curling around the hilt of a silver dagger. "Just a little hunting. No need to be alarmed."

"Be careful. The Houston house thinks you're a mild-mannered scholar on vacation."

"Bollocks," Rhys muttered. "Goodbye, Max."

He hung up before his brother could say another word. He tossed the phone in the passenger seat and closed the car door. The

Grigori and the woman had disappeared to the back of the parking lot. Rhys hadn't noticed him arriving in a car, but perhaps he'd convinced the woman to give him a ride to a more secluded location where he could feed from her.

Grigori were soul hungry. Human mythology called them incubi or vampires. Even cannibals. They fed from the soul energy that all human beings possessed, though most preferred women. Women they could lure with their looks and their scent. They were born predators, dark sons of heaven made to seduce and feed.

In a shadowed corner of the back parking lot, Rhys saw the Grigori pressing the woman against her car, kissing her neck as the her head was thrown back. She was panting, her breasts heaving in a macabre imitation of pleasure. In reality, there could be no pleasure for her because the Grigori's bare hands were pressed to her stomach and back, his touch robbing the waitress of her free will. She was putty in the creature's hands, willing to do anything he asked, his touch more effective than a drug.

Rhys approached quietly, but the Grigori must have sensed him. The creature spun, keeping one hand on the woman.

"You," he hissed.

"If you were smart," Rhys said, "you'd already be running."

The Grigori's eyes were cold and blank. No hint of conscience warmed them. "She wanted me. She said yes."

"She doesn't know what you are." Rhys glanced at the woman. Her eyes were still closed. She was still panting. Her moans of pleasure scraped against his ears like nails on slate. "Get away from her."

The Grigori hesitated, his eyes narrowed in growing panic. Rhys noticed the second the man decided to run. He broke away from the woman and lunged to the left, dashing between cars as Rhys caught the human woman and laid her on the ground. Then he shot to his feet and ran after the man who was running toward Kirby Drive.

The older waitress walked out of the restaurant just as Rhys ran past.

"Your friend is in the back," he yelled. "She's hurt!"

Rhys left the humans and ran, waiting for the traffic to pass so he could follow the Grigori. Cars honked and drivers rolled down their windows to yell as he ran.

There.

Rhys caught a glimpse of the monster as he darted between two parked cars in a multi-story car park. The Grigori might have been running to his own vehicle or simply trying to lose Rhys. Either way, the creature was going to die.

He paused when he entered the garage, brushing a thumb over the talesm prim on his left wrist and waiting for his senses to sharpen. In seconds, his eyes adjusted to the darkness, his heart rate steadied, and his ears picked up the footsteps running up the ramp and toward the roof. Rhys followed the sound, drawing the silver stiletto from its hidden sheath and gripping it tightly.

He reached the top of the garage and was barely breathing harder. The moon had disappeared behind a blue fog that drifted over the city, but yellow lights buzzed on the roof, casting strange overlapping shadows between the parked cars.

There were several rows of parked cars and trucks. Rhys walked among them deliberately, waiting for a sound, a scent, anything. He sorted through the acrid smell of burning sulfur, exhaust, and mold.

There.

A row of pickup trucks caught his eye, every one of them a potential hiding place for the Grigori.

"Who do you belong to?" Rhys asked. "Who commands you, Grigori?"

A creak near the blue truck.

Not the blue, the red.

"There are ways to live without killing," Rhys said.

A shuffle and a break in the silence. The Grigori took a running leap from the top of the parking garage to the office building on the other side of the alley.

"Are you joking?" Rhys grumbled. He hated to jump and he didn't particularly like heights. "You fecking knob!" Rhys grit his teeth and ran toward the edge, concentrating on the burst of magical energy as he leapt into the darkness.

A fall from four stories wouldn't kill him, but it would hurt like hell.

He landed and rolled on the gravel roof of the office building just in time to see the Grigori slip over the side. Rhys needed to get to the ground fast. He spotted a drain pipe and ran toward it, shimmying down the dirty pipe until he was close enough to fall. He ran around the corner of the building just in time to see the Grigori dangle from the fire escape and drop.

Rhys grabbed him by the neck while he was still catching his balance and shoved him face first against the brick wall of the office building.

The man was smaller than he'd appeared on the run. Rhys was tall, over six foot, with a runner's build and a long reach. Far from bulky, Rhys dwarfed him.

He gripped him by the neck. "Who do you belong to?"

The man's shoulders slumped. "Bozidar."

"The archangel?" Not likely. Bozidar's sons would have more natural magic than this. "How many women have you fed from like the waitress?"

The man froze. "Not enough." Then he turned and snapped his teeth at Rhys's left wrist in a last ditch effort to damage the scribe's magic.

Without a second thought, Rhys plunged the silver stiletto into the base of the Grigori's neck and waited. Within seconds, the body began to shimmer and disintegrate. Rhys stepped back and wiped the dust from his blade before he returned it to the sheath, watching silently as dust rose through the heavy night sky, disappearing into the darkness and mist.

Under his breath, Rhys said a prayer. He'd slain a son of the angels. Fallen angels, yes. But the same blood ran in his veins. The same magic fueled him. Grigori were the dark shadow of the Irin. Without knowledge and training, scribes would turn feral too.

The lone Grigori had been no challenge, and Rhys felt no satisfaction in the kill, no sense of righteous anger or vengeance.

Bozidar.

The archangel from St. Louis. It hadn't been the whole truth, but there had been a ring to it. Perhaps the young man had belonged to one of Bozidar's lesser Fallen allies. He'd report the incident to his watcher and let Malachi decide if he wanted to pass the information along.

After all, Rhys was nothing more than a visiting scholar from Istanbul.

Hardly a threat at all.

Rhys slept until noon the next day, waking only when the housekeeper tapped on his door. He'd checked with his Spanish passport, so Rhys called out in Spanish, asking for a few minutes more. He threw off the sheet that covered him and took a moment to enjoy the cool breeze on his bare chest. He rubbed the unmarked skin over his heart, wondering for the thousandth time what it would feel like to put a needle into it. His first marks had been made at the age of thirteen by his father, a stern man who impressed on Rhys the importance of history and legacy and tradition. Those talesm ran down his back, covering the magic his mother had spoken over him from the time of his birth.

"When you find your mate, then you will know true wisdom."

His parents still lived, still tended the library in Glast as every scribe in his family had done since the beginning of time. Rhys was a direct descendant of Gabriel's line in Glastonbury. His father had been the chief archivist as his grandfather had been. Rhys's children

—if he ever had any—would be expected to follow in that line. In the early days, the scribes in his family only took trained Irina librarians as mates, so the Great Library at Glast had been one of the rare joined archives of their race. Rhys's grandfather had met his reshon and broken that tradition, but no one had blamed him for it. A reshon was a rare and beautiful gift, the single perfect soul created by heaven to be your equal.

Rhys still hoped for a mate someday. A reshon was likely too much to ask. Of course, it wasn't easy finding any mate when eighty percent of the women in your race had been killed.

He hadn't given up hope. Not exactly. After all, all of his brothers in Istanbul had found mates. Malachi, his new watcher, had mated with Ava, an American with unique Grigori blood. Leo had also mated a kareshta singer, and Rhys was fairly sure Max and Renata were finally together, though the cagey Irina had led his brother on a fifteen year chase.

There was hope. Probably. If those bastards could find women to put up with them, there had to be someone who could keep his interest for more than a single conversation.

Rhys groaned and rolled out of bed. He could feel the onerous heat pressing against the windows and creeping under the door. He showered and threw on his spare change of clothes, unconcerned about covering his talesm that morning. Americans were easy about such things. Tattoos were so common now, he'd noticed professionals and grandmothers inked with them. The neat rows of intricate writing covering his arms were unlikely to raise more than a casual interest.

He stood at the door of his motel room, enjoying the brief moment of being perspiration-free before he slid on his sunglasses and walked outside.

Ah yes. Covered in sweat again.

Walking quickly down the stairs, he found the compact blue rental car and threw his backpack in the passenger seat. Then he drove two blocks away and returned the car at the rental agency before he called for a taxi. He took that car to another hotel and walked from there to a national car rental.

If he was going to take a road trip, he wanted the right car and it needed far better air-conditioning than the blue compact. He took off his sunglasses and scanned the lot.

A salesman walked up to him. "Can I help you, sir?"

Rhys spotted it, a silver Dodge Challenger with tan leather interior. "That one." He walked over to look inside.

Leg room. Glorious, glorious leg room.

"The Challenger?" the man appeared to be excited. "An excellent choice. It has—"

"Would it be possible to return it in New Orleans?"

"Yes, sir. There would be an additional charge."

"Not a problem."

He slid his sunglasses back on. Yes, this one would do nicely.

Within minutes, he was driving on Interstate 10, "Way Down We Go" blaring from the speakers, crossing the channel and heading east to New Orleans to find a legend lost for three hundred years.

———

For more information about THE SEEKER and other works of fiction, please subscribe to my newsletter or visit ElizabethHunterWrites.com.

ACKNOWLEDGMENTS

I'd like to thank everyone who encouraged me to write this story, especially Grace Draven, Thea Harrison, and Jeffe Kennedy. The Storm originally appeared in the *Amid the Winter Snow* anthology with stories from these three other talented authors. I'd been debating how or if I even wanted to tell Max and Renata's story, and these three ladies gave me the push I needed.

I want to give a special thanks to my wonderful editor, Anne Victory. Her participation on this project came at a painful personal time, and I cannot express how much it meant to me that she was willing to work on this book. Anne, so much love to you and your family. I am honored to not only call you an editor, but a friend.

I also want to thank all the Hunters in my reader group who were so enthusiastic to read about this prickly pair. Many Irina stories are hard to tell, and losing her soul mate made Renata an especially hard subject.

And as always, love and gratitude to my family. Though we aren't always close geographically, we hold each other in our hearts. You are all home to me, no matter which continent you currently reside on.

For Renata, like so many who have suffered real loss, the only way to move forward from a painful past is to find meaning and purpose in the present.

To everyone who has suffered loss—big and small—I pray that you have the audacity to hope, the bravery to love, and the faith to continue on your journey.

ABOUT THE AUTHOR

ELIZABETH HUNTER is a *USA Today* and international best-selling author of romance, contemporary fantasy, and paranormal mystery. Based in Central California, she travels extensively to write fantasy fiction exploring world mythologies, history, and the universal bonds of love, friendship, and family. She has published over thirty works of fiction and sold over a million books worldwide. She is the author of Love Stories on 7th and Main, the Elemental Legacy series, the Irin Chronicles, the Cambio Springs Mysteries, and other works of fiction.

ElizabethHunterWrites.com

ALSO BY ELIZABETH HUNTER

The Irin Chronicles

The Scribe

The Singer

The Secret

The Staff and the Blade

The Silent

The Storm

The Seeker (Summer 2018)

The Elemental Mysteries

A Hidden Fire

This Same Earth

The Force of Wind

A Fall of Water

All the Stars Look Down (novella)

The Elemental World

Building From Ashes

Waterlocked (novella)

Blood and Sand

The Bronze Blade (novella)

The Scarlet Deep

Beneath a Waning Moon (novella)

A Stone-Kissed Sea

The Elemental Legacy

Shadows and Gold

Imitation and Alchemy

Omens and Artifacts

Midnight Labyrinth

Blood Apprentice (Winter 2018)

The Cambio Springs Series

Long Ride Home (short story)

Shifting Dreams

Five Mornings (short story)

Desert Bound

Waking Hearts

Contemporary Romance

The Genius and the Muse

7th and Main

INK

HOOKED (Winter 2019)